FIGHTING FOR MONSTERS

FALLING FOR THE ENEMY (BOOK TWO)

LUNA PIERCE

FIGHTING FOR MONSTERS

Who you were yesterday does not dictate who you can become tomorrow.

I
WREN

The musty air assaults me with its vile and putrid stench.

Piss, no doubt, and *other* bodily functions. The scent of blood lingers, and the coppery taste of it coats my mouth.

My head throbs and it takes all my strength to sit upright.

I blink through the darkness, and my eyes desperately scan for a sign, any indication of where I am.

But even with the absence of a flashing sign alerting me to my whereabouts, my gut knows either way. I'm in hell, or at least, a version of it in this realm.

A place that is inescapable.

Rock Bridge.

Once you step foot in here—as a prisoner—freedom becomes a thing of the past.

The weight of that hits much harder now that I'm on the opposite end of things for a change.

How many creatures have I brought here over the years? All have met the same tortured end—thanks to me.

I was proud. I was celebrated. And now, I am locked behind the same walls I once put those creatures behind; every ounce of my liberty stripped from me.

In one sheer moment, I have become nothing.

And for what?

My palm rests against my chest as the ache of a memory crashes over me.

Wes, helpless and writhing in agony, his arm outstretched toward mine, his lips muttering an apology that he never should have spoken. One I wish I could erase from history. If only I could have willed him to stay concealed with Bo and Dash.

Then he would be safe, and it would only be my life on the line.

I swallow the cruel reality of not knowing what fate has in store for him, and there not being a damn thing I can do about it. Not when I'm locked in this fucking cage.

Cold metal shackles clamp down on both of my wrists, hindering my ability to access any of the magic within my body.

I'd pry at them, but I know better than to expect them to come off without the key.

I might be powerless, but that doesn't mean I'm

completely defenseless. I'm trained in combat and have a handful of skills that could never be stripped so easily.

Still, I'd rather be at full strength than thwarted by these magical restraints.

"Fuck," I mutter, rising to my feet.

Keeping my hands out in front of me, I feel along the brick wall, carefully skimming my fingers in search of anything to help familiarize myself with this place.

"Why is it so fucking dark in here?" I ask myself.

I've been in here a matter of hours, and I'm already acting like a crazy person.

I stop when I catch the sound of a dainty voice floating toward me.

"Hello?" I say into the darkness. "Is someone in here?"

"Shh," the person replies. "Down here."

I cower my aching body toward the source of the whispers.

"This way," she guides me.

I press my core flat against the concrete floor and fumble with the tiny opening separating our chambers. Small sturdy rods ensure that we both stay put in our isolated spaces.

"It's no use," she tells me. "Not like you'd do any better over here than in there."

I sigh and scoot onto my butt, pressing my side on the wall. "How long have you been here?"

The girl considers the question for a long moment before answering. "A while."

No doubt one of my kind that put her in that position.

With the suppression of my powers, I can't access my hunter radar to tell what she is, but if I had to guess, she seems no different than me. What could she have done to deserve being locked up like this?

A ripple of pain abruptly rushes through me. I gasp and clutch my hand over my torso to try to locate the source of the profound brutality. I stifle a moan and hunch over as another fierce lash strikes.

"Are you okay?" the girl asks.

"I...I don't know. Is this...?" I struggle to get out the last word before I'm struck again. "Normal?" I finally blurt out.

How can I be tortured without someone here doing it to me? Even magic has its bounds.

"You're alone, aren't you?"

I grip the wall and force myself to my feet. Reaching blindly, I throw my arms around the space, slamming them into the bricks but nothing else. I kick a bucket, knocking it over and sending it clattering. I push through the pain to verify that unless someone outmaneuvered me in complete silence, I am the only one in these confines.

Using my instincts to guide me back, I settle onto the floor near the opening between our cells. "What's with the fucking dark?"

"I think they do it to disorient us." The girl's metal chains clang as she repositions herself. "There's no pattern to when they blast us with light, but shield your eyes when it happens. It's bright as hell at first."

Hell, that's for damn sure. I've never been to the realm ruled by Balial or his brothers, but I can only imagine the similarities given the stories I've been told.

I double over, muttering obscenities as another round of pain strikes my core.

Fingers, cold and small, wrap themselves around my forearm.

Startled, I want to pull away, but the agony keeps me rooted in place. I allow the stranger to comfort me because I can't exactly do much of anything else.

A moment passes along with the discomfort, and the girl pulls her hand back through the small opening.

"Why did you do that?" I ask her.

The girl inhales deeply and lets out a hasty breath. "Us girls have to stick together."

She doesn't even know me and she's already shown me extreme kindness. If she was aware of the truth, she probably wouldn't want anything to do with me. I am the enemy after all. Especially in a place like this, when it's because of me and my kind that these people are here.

People. At the end of the day, they're no different than me, not if you really think about it. All of us fighting to stay alive—killing each other to survive. It's no wonder this realm has gone to complete shit when its main agenda is war.

My usual distaste for their kind doesn't come, only

continually reinforcing my newfound understanding that maybe I've had it wrong all along. I've spent my entire life waging an unwinnable war, and for what? To be stabbed in the back the second I disobey an order.

Turning to the wall, I mutter, "What's your name?"

She hesitates, quite like how she did when I questioned how long she had been here. "You promise you won't tell anyone?"

The mark on my neck burns, a permanent reminder of a life I will never know.

"I promise." And although we've only just met, I mean those two words. I've never been the trusting kind, but where has that ever gotten me?

"Franny," she finally confides in me.

"Franny," I repeat. "My name is Wren, and one way or another, I will get us out of here."

How? I have no fucking clue, but I refuse to die in this shithole.

A soft double knock sounds from her room.

"Quick, shut your eyes," Franny urges me.

I comply, the light blasting my face a second later. The heat of it scorches my face and slowly dims down into a tolerable warmth, which continues to fade.

"You should be safe to open them now."

"How did you know?" An uneasy suspicion rises within me.

She does that thing where she wavers again, no doubt wondering if she can put her trust in me. "There's a guard...he tries to warn me sometimes."

Perhaps we could use that to our advantage.

I allow my eyes to adjust to the yellowish illumination in my cell. It's exactly how I imagined. Four solid brick walls with one heavily armored door posted across from me. An identical small opening connects each room to the next at the base of the floor and wall. There's a grated drain in the middle of the room with a slope coming off each corner. The only luxury in here, the bucket I had kicked over, sits haphazardly in the place it landed.

I scan the ceiling, squinting through the light but not finding anything noteworthy.

Sighing, I hobble over to the door and examine its solid nature. I skim my fingers along every inch of it, pushing and poking and wishing for even the smallest weakness.

Commotion from outside my room sparks my interest, and I do what I can to peer through a small crack on the hinge of the door.

My heart stutters, my mouth gapes open, and my sights settle on the last face I saw before being brought here.

Wes. Beaten and bloodied, worse than he was then.

I pound my fist against the cold, hard surface and scream. "What did you do to him?"

But it's no use, the guards dragging his body don't give a shit about me or what I have to say. Instead, they continue on their path, opening the cell next to mine and throwing Wes inside.

His body lands with a thud on the floor, followed by a groan that escapes him.

I drop onto my chest and scamper toward the small opening between our rooms. "Wes," I whisper. I painfully shove my hand through the bars, my skin scraping against the surface, and reach with intense desperation toward him. "Wes," I repeat. "I'm here." But what good will that do him? I'm the reason he's in this mess in the first place.

It's my fault. All of this is my fault.

Wes shifts toward me like he finally realizes who's calling out to him. He inches his weakened frame in my direction.

My breath catches at witnessing him this weak. How could they have done this to such a powerful being?

He extends his hand, his fingers barely grazing mine as he collapses in place.

I shove myself further through the meager opening, ignoring the sound filling my room. Metal creaking, voices that follow. None of it is as important as making sure he knows I'm here, that I'm sorry, that I would do anything to make this right.

But that time never comes.

My ankles are gripped by strong hands, and I'm yanked away from the opening, my flesh torn away from the abrupt motion against the bars.

I immediately flip onto my back, drag my knee to my chest, and kick the guard directly in the stomach, knocking him from his feet. I hop onto my own and slam my fist into the throat of the other nameless guard.

"Fucking bitch," he blurts out while clutching himself.

A smile creeps across my face as another guard enters my cell. This one with a long metal rod that sizzles with energy.

Fuck.

He jabs the thing into my side before I can jump out of the way.

My vision blurs and my body rattles with the electricity now surging into me.

"I will make you pay for this," I say through gasping breaths once the jolts pass through me.

I will make them *all* pay.

2

BO

"I can't just fucking sit here and do nothing."

Dash glances behind him and then at me. "I'm not asking you to, but I'm pretty sure we can't help them if we're dead."

I narrow my gaze at him. "Don't be so sure of yourself, that's kind of your special talent."

"Great." Dash throws up his arms. "The only thing I'm good for is dying. How do you expect that to come in handy?"

I shrug. "We'll figure something out."

A branch breaks in the distance, drawing our attention in its direction.

We're stuck in enemy territory with no way out, and Wren and Wes have been beaten and brought to the worst possible place—Rock Bridge. A place that, in all my years, I've never heard of anyone making it out of alive. A place our people were taken to years ago. I sort of accepted the fact that I would never see them again, but now that Wes and Wren have met that same fate, it's not as easy to stomach.

It shouldn't bother me. She *is* the enemy after all; but deep down she's so much more than that. Not just to me, but to Wes and Dash, too. I can't explain it—and I'm not even sure I want to. But I cannot allow that place to consume her, too. Maybe it's the mark I left on her neck drawing me to her. Maybe it's because, from the moment I saw her, I haven't been able to get her off my mind. I thought it was the hatred that fueled my incessant thoughts. But now I'm not really sure of anything.

And as for Wes, well, he's been like a brother to me. I can't just let him rot in that place.

But how do I get him out—get her out—when it could be the most impossible thing ever?

"I don't think we're safe here," Dash whispers.

"No shit." I nudge his shoulder. "We have to keep moving."

Our distance from the place causes another issue. I marked Wren, and if the two of us are separated by much space, a beacon alerting demons that she's fresh for the taking will go off. And unless I'm heavily mistaken, she's surrounded by the likes of them in that hellhole.

I thought I was doing the right thing at the time—marking her in order to keep her close.

But it very well could be the thing that gets her

killed.

How do I keep myself safe when doing so could risk her life?

"You're telling me you don't have any other powers?" I glance over at Dash as we run through the densely packed forest to find another spot to catch our breath and regroup.

Maybe eventually we'll come up with some kind of plan.

"I...I don't think so." Dash stays near my side.

I recall the time I've spent with him over the years and try to pinpoint anything that could be of use. He's not any good in battle, although on occasion he's held his own. There's nothing remarkable about winning a fight every now and then, though.

"A phoenix is a bird...you're telling me you can't fly?"

"Pretty sure you'd know if I could fly," Dash quips. He throws his arms out to the side. "Do you see any wings, Bo?"

Despite the running for our lives, I chuckle. "No, all I see is an idiot flapping his arms."

"I just found out what I am, cut me some slack."

He's right. I've had powers my entire life and still come across new skills from time to time. Hell, my species doesn't even have a name—one that I'm aware of, at least. All I know is that I'm an alpha, the last of my kind, which gives me a superior strength over pretty much all other demons. All of them except for Wes. His hound supersedes any power known in this realm.

And here he is, locked away like a fucking idiot. If he would have just stayed put, all three of us could have figured out how to rescue Wren together. Instead, Dash and I are left up shit's creek with no paddle to figure this mess out and try to stay alive in the process.

"We're going to have to circle closer," I tell Dash when I notice the tether connecting me to Wren tugs tighter.

"Why? What's wrong?"

What *isn't* wrong at this point? We're basically running around the same confined area and dodging random hunters. Hunters who will no doubt stop at nothing to either kill us or bring us in to potentially meet a much worse fate. But if I get inside those walls, maybe it'll give me a better chance of getting to Wren. Maybe I could free her and find a way to get myself and Wes out.

I shake my head. What am I thinking? That's a suicide mission. And yet, it's incredibly enticing. How did I go from wanting to rip her throat out to risking my own life for hers in a matter of a week? What the fuck is wrong with me?

Dash grips my shoulder and stops me in place. "Dude, talk to me." He slaps my face. "Snap out of it."

"What?" I huff.

"You've got that murderous look on your ugly mug. The one you get right before you do something stupid."

I deadpan. "I don't know what you're talking about."

"You care, and it's eating you alive." Dash surprises me with his bluntness.

I blink down at him. "Do not."

He runs his hand through his red hair. "I care about her, too, and Wes."

"Only because you slept with her," I mouth off.

Dash leans up against a tree and catches his breath. He grins and his cheeks redden. "You're jealous."

"Am not."

"Whatever. You don't have to admit it for it to be true." Dash pulls off his backpack and reaches in to pull out a hunk of bread. He bites off a piece of it and throws the rest at me. "And for the record, I cared about her before I had sex with her."

I chew the bread slowly and attempt to savor the dwindling rations we have. It won't be long until we'll have to start getting dangerously close to the hunters if we want to feed ourselves. We're already running on fumes, no sense in dwindling away completely if we want to be of use to Wes and Wren. It'll be a necessary risk if we intend on staying alive. Nothing we haven't done before, although usually we aren't stuck behind enemy lines with no chance of escaping.

I swallow the mouthful and keep my gaze trained on the distance. "Why?"

"You already know." Dash sighs. "She's special."

"I refuse to accept that." I plop my ass onto a fallen log and stretch my arms. "*Special*, seriously? You buy that?"

Dash seems to consider my words. "Yeah." He rubs the toe of his shoe into the ground. "It doesn't have to make sense if it *feels* right. Listen, nothing about my life adds up. Not why I have no memory, why I was left out here alone, how I came back from the dead. Questioning those things has only added to the heartache, so you better believe the first time something *truly* good comes along, I'm going to just roll with it." He pauses for a second. "Did she cast a spell on me? On us? Is she going to be our demise? I don't fucking know. But honestly, I don't care. Not if for the first time in my life, from what I can remember, I've felt something that resembles happiness. And you'd be lying if you said you didn't feel that connection with her, too. We already know Wes does. Maybe that's why you two found me instead of someone else. Maybe our fates were decided long ago, and we're just now lining the puzzle pieces into place. Or maybe I'm a fool who's drunk on the idea of possibilities that could never happen."

Every single word he speaks somehow makes complete and utter sense, despite it making none at all. I don't know how Wren has managed to wrap us all around her finger with such ease, but the idea of not ever seeing her again pains me in a way I can't begin to describe. I'm not meant to have *feelings* like this. I never have, and the more they fester, the angrier I get at not having control over them.

Dash smiles to himself. "There's no denying how great she is. She's funny, smart, strong as hell, and stunning. I've never met anyone like her in my limited time in this realm."

I exhale and tuck a strand of my black hair behind my ear. "Neither have I." And I've been alive a lot longer than Dash has, even with his memory problems making his experience much shorter.

"So, you admit it?" Dash raises a brow at me.

"That you're an idiot? Yeah." I throw a rock at him and stand, dusting my pants off.

"I see the way you look at her. How protective you are of her. That guy at the tavern. Any other instance you would have blown someone like him off..."

I scan the vicinity and try to pick up any nearby hunters that might be on our tails. "You're pushing it, Dash."

"But I'm not wrong."

I stretch my neck from side to side, cracking it with each movement. "She's infuriating."

And I can't get enough.

Dash swings his backpack over his shoulder and secures it in place. "She's the only woman who's ever stood her ground against you, and I think it drives you crazy."

I ignore how right he is and shift the focus of our

conversation to more pressing matters. "We need to find shelter and wait out dusk. We can move more freely at night."

He may not have night vision, but I do, and we must take any advantage we can over the hunters.

3
WES

I grit my jaw and take every ounce of pain they unleash on me.

"You will talk, one way or another." The man slams his fist across my face.

My blood splatters against his shirt and trickles down onto the floor, along with everywhere else gravity demands. Down my chin, my neck, onto my chest.

Even if I wanted to talk, there's nothing of value I have to add. He's asking questions I don't have the answers to.

The guy yanks the collar of my shirt and tugs me toward him, despite the fact that I'm secured to this chair he's strapped me to. "Where is the rest of your kind?"

I glare up at him through my lashes. "Go to hell." I shouldn't, but I suck in a breath and spit in his face. There are no others, and there haven't been for as long as I can remember. I was orphaned from birth—my parents were killed by hunters, and I was left to die in my mother's womb. I should have died along with them, but I wasn't that lucky. No, I was cut out by a woman who would assume the maternal role and do her best to raise me as her own. I don't blame her for her kindness, but knowing the outcome of both of our fates, it may have served us both better if she let me perish that day.

"I can't wait until I get the order to gut you." The man wipes at the blood-covered spittle on his cheeks. "I will take great pleasure in making you suffer."

He isn't already doing so?

"Are we done here, or do you need to get your rocks off a little more?" I ask the sick fuck.

"Oh, I haven't even gotten started." The man draws back his fist, this time flipping something metal onto his knuckles.

"Enough," another guard calls out as he stalks into the room. He grabs my tormentor's shoulder and reels him back. "I said *enough*."

The newcomer is easily half the age of the arrogant brute but somehow has authority over him. It takes him a second to get the guy to snap into place, but once he does, he huffs and storms out of the room. The new guy watches him intensely, not taking his gaze off him until he's shut the door. Only then does he look down at me.

"What? You ready to take your turn?" I reposition

my tied hands and straighten myself in the chair, preparing myself for whatever is to come next.

Instead, he walks around me and kneels. "I'm here to escort you back to your holding cell." He unlatches my cuffs from the chair but keeps them secured behind me.

I consider the possibilities. Could I break one of my wrists and maneuver my hands to the frontal position before he could stop me? Or perhaps shove him with brute force and knock him down and attempt to locate the key to my magical restraint? Then I could finally unleash my hound on him and the rest of this wretched place.

Countless scenarios run through my mind, but all of them end up with eventual failure. There's no telling what kind of magical hold this place has on me; no telling the number of guards posted outside this door or along my path to freedom. The simple fact that I haven't had any contact with my hound since stepping foot in this place is enough to cause me to tread lightly. In all my life I've never been this separated from him. His typical obnoxious and annoying banter has been replaced with a sort of shadow...a ghost where he once was. It's unfamiliar and completely foreign, and I'd be lying if I said it wasn't alarming. Did he distance himself to keep us both safe? To keep our identity concealed? Is it possible that this prison did something terrible to him? What could've caused my other self to disappear?

What kind of twisted hell hole is this place?

"Where did they take the girl?" I ask, knowing damn well I shouldn't. The question burns through me and forces itself out of my mouth.

The guard pauses on our way to the door. He leans in a little closer like he's about to tell me a secret.

I hold my breath in anticipation, a million different outcomes that will wreck me all the same. Even with my hound's absence, my desire for her remains unchanged. If anything, it's heightened now that she somewhat reciprocated my feelings back at her place—kissing me with an intensity to spark a forest fire. And the idea of her being put through the same torment they're inflicting on me, or something worse...

"They're trying to get you to crack," he finally tells me.

"Crack?"

"They want to know where the rest of your kind are."

Again, with the shit I can't help them with.

He continues, "Once they realize one way or another, they'll be done with both of you. If I were you, I'd stop being so convincing that you don't know anything."

"Why are you telling me this?" I scan his features, noting how weirdly soft and sincere they are. He reminds me a bit of Dash and how innocent he is on the surface. Or well, as a whole—that guy is the best of us all. So very human, despite him being a rarity to this world. A fucking phoenix.

The man opens his mouth to speak but the handle on the door wobbles and creaks. He stutters for a second and mutters, "Follow my lead."

The thick metal door opens and another guard, wearing the same generic black uniform as the others, appears on the other side. "Oh, didn't realize this one was occupied." He averts his gaze to the floor once his eyes lock onto the badges pinned to the lapel of the man holding my cuffed arms. "Sir," he adds.

"Out of my way," the guy commands while tugging me with him. He yanks on my arm and shoves me through the doorway.

The other guy steps aside and keeps his head down the whole time.

I steal a glance at his strange obedience as we round the corner into an empty corridor.

The man loosens his grip on me once we're out of sight. "I'm not like the rest of them."

"I've gathered that," I whisper quiet enough that he can still hear me.

"There are other guards posted in your hallway, so you need to play along."

"What's your name?" I ask him before we've gone too far.

He slows his walk for a split second to say, "Everest, but you must never call me by it."

Just like he mentioned, two chattering guards are

down the next pathway. The duo immediately stand alert and shut their mouths, scampering to look as on-duty as possible.

I avoid meeting their glares and stay focused on the cobbled stone of the floor below my feet.

One of them clears their throat, "Do you need assistance, sir?"

Everest tugs on my arm. "I've already broken this one for the day." He nods toward my door. "Open that and step away."

The little bitch boy runs ahead to comply with the order and then goes back to his post.

Everest stops us in front of the open door and fumbles with my cuffs, freeing my hands from behind my back. The metal shackles remain on my wrists, suppressing my magic, but it's a welcomed relief not to have them tied in such an uncomfortable position. Especially during the pathetic attempts that guard used to *break* me.

"I'm going to shove you," he mumbles quietly.

With his warning, I dramatically fall into the holding cell, dropping onto my knees with a grunt, performing this strange role play with a man I know next to nothing about. I can use any help I can get, no matter where it comes from. My only concern is that he's playing me like a fool.

The metal scrapes against the floor as the door shuts behind me, sealing me into my confinement. I wait until it's latched in place to lift myself up and hurry over to the tiny opening between cells.

"Wren," I whisper into the hole. I press my bloodied face on the concrete and frantically try to peer into the last place I saw her.

My heart aches when my eyes continue to scan the emptiness on the other side of this wall. Her touch is like a fever dream that has me concerned I made the whole thing up as some sort of coping mechanism. It's been at least a day since she called out to me and reached her dainty hand through and grazed her fingers against mine. It took all my strength to drag myself closer to her, but by the time I made it there, I was too late. Someone had come into her room and viciously yanked her away from me.

She had screamed and called out but there was nothing I could do. I slammed my fists into the wall until my knuckles and hands were coated with blood and plasma and dirt. The pain was nothing compared to what I felt inside...at what I continue to feel at having put her in this position. I never meant for any of this to happen. The whole reason I saved her from that abandoned warehouse was because I couldn't fathom watching her die. My soul wouldn't allow it. But little did my soul know, everything that would follow would only continue to put her in danger, and it would all be my fault.

I could've saved her and let her go. Why did I have to bring her back to our home? A home full of her enemies. Why did I have to be selfish? Why did I refuse to see any other alternative other than keeping her nearby? Why did I continue to keep her powers at bay knowing what a dangerous world we live in? I was too much of a coward. Too afraid that she would leave given the chance. My selfishness is what got us in this mess. And I can only imagine the shit Dash and Bo are going through trying to figure out how the hell to get out of this enemy territory.

I've doomed us all.

Even my hound.

Because of something the fucking fates decided long ago.

I settle against the uncomfortable hardness of the wall that's separating me from where Wren once was. I sigh, looking my hands over front to back. The healing process is considerably much slower than it typically is. It's almost as though these magical restraints have left me as nothing more than a shell of a weak and fragile human. Everything aches. I'm not sure there's an inch of me that doesn't have something wrong with it. I'm used to pain, quite fond of it, actually. I'm just not accustomed to it lingering in this capacity. Although, I am grateful for its constant reminder of how badly I royally fucked things up. I deserve no less than this torment. My only wish is that she's safe from whatever this place has in store for us. I would allow someone to slowly rip my skin from my body if it meant getting her out of here.

Everest told me that they would do anything they

could to get me to crack. Unfortunately, there's nothing to give. I have no information to exchange for her freedom. I could give them something false to buy us some time, but how long would that last? And would the punishment that would follow be worth it?

He seems to have authority here, maybe I could cut a deal with him to set her free. Or maybe he's just playing a really solid game of good cop/bad cop to trick me into telling him whatever these sick fucks want to know.

I lean my head against the wall and draw in a breath. My torso aches with each inch it expands.

"You in there?" I mutter to no one other than myself. My hound refuses to answer and I'm not convinced it's because he can't...maybe he just won't.

4
WREN

"Wes," I plead while gripping his hand tighter.

He's on his side, his blood-covered face toward the small opening between our rooms.

I stare intently and wait for the steady rise and fall of his chest. I don't dare exhale until I see the smallest movement, denying my fear that the worst has happened.

I lay on my own side while keeping my hand shoved through the bars and loosen my hold on him. I keep it there but decide to stop trying to wake him. It must have been difficult for him to fall asleep given the conditions—he should rest while he can.

Studying the cuts littering what I can make out of his body, I grow concerned about his lack of healing. Usually, those types of things would have fixed themselves by now, but instead, he looks terrible. Dark lines crease his brow and dirt and dried blood touch nearly every inch of his skin. A purple bruise covers his cheek, and his lip is split on the bottom.

What are these assholes doing to him?

I bring my finger to my own mouth, skimming it over the fresh wound that still oozes blood. They worked me over pretty well, too, but I won't be broken that easily. Physical torture is nothing I'm unfamiliar with. I was trained to withstand this kind of torment.

Sighing, I wiggle my hand under Wes's and cup his large palm. I close my eyes and allow this temporary moment to comfort me. I can't say I've been in worse situations than this, but I've escaped death enough times to know I need to gain my strength if I want to make it out of this one, too.

I don't dream, and I'm not entirely sure I fall asleep at all. Perhaps I was stuck in that sort of in-between of consciousness. Either way, my attention clings to the cracked voice of the man across from me.

"Wren," he breathes. "Is that really you?"

As if I'm what, a figment of his imagination?

"In the flesh." I blink my vision straight and take in the sight of his beautiful and tortured face. "You look like shit."

Somehow, this garners a grin out of him. "Thanks, so do you."

I stay on my side, my arm outstretched through the meager opening. I squeeze his hand despite the incredibly uncomfortable position I'm in. Tingles float from my fingertips up to my shoulder. "Why aren't you healing?" I ask him.

His smile fades and he shakes his head. "I don't know." Wes wiggles his wrist. "Must be these."

"I'm sorry," we both say at the very same time.

Our brows furrow, almost like we're mimicking each other's expressions.

He runs his thumb along the outside of the wound on my hand. "You have nothing to be sorry for."

"I'm the reason we're in this mess." If I would have come up with a better plan this wouldn't have happened. If I wouldn't have underestimated how vicious my superiors were maybe I would've anticipated this. Maybe if I didn't work for the fucking bad guy.

This whole time I thought I was on the right side of the war. But now I'm not so sure. I was always taught that demons and their bringers were the evil in this world. From my current position, it kind of looks like I was wrong. That's not to say that demons aren't bad, it's just that...maybe hunters are getting more credit than they deserve.

"You're joking, right?" Wes stares through the opening at me. "Everything leading up to this moment was my fault. What happened at that warehouse. Bringing you to my home. Allowing Bo to mark you and pretending I did any of this for any reason other than the most obvious one."

I swallow down the lump of emotions bubbling up. "You did it for your people. To get them back."

Wes steadies his gaze. "You don't get it, do you? I did it for *you*. Because I'm selfish and couldn't stand to let you go."

"You know nothing about me," I say, like it'll somehow convince him otherwise.

"That's what I kept telling myself. But I knew deep down, in a visceral way, that I would follow you to the ends of this world and whatever comes next. My hound made damn sure I knew that, too."

"And what does he have to say now?"

His jaw clenches and his nostrils flare slightly while he averts his gaze. "I don't know."

"He's having second thoughts?" I try to make sense of what he's saying.

"No."

"Then what do you mean?"

"I..." Wes chews at the inside of his lip.

It suddenly dawns on me. Wes isn't healing. His powers are suppressed. I haven't seen the glowing red orbs of his eyes since we got here. Not a trace of his fiery energy. "He's gone?"

"I'm not sure where he is."

"How is that even possible?" I know this place has control over our magic, but never in my wildest dreams would I have imagined they'd be capable of blocking such a commanding beast.

"I'm sorry I can't heal you." Wes flashes his gaze to the cut on my hand. He brings it closer to him and presses his lips along the edge. "You don't deserve this."

"It's kind of funny," I find myself saying.

"What?"

I grin at him. "This." I give his hand a gentle squeeze. "I thought you hated my guts a week ago. I mean, hell, *I* hated *your* guts a week ago. I wanted to kill you...and Bo." I shrug and add, "Dash a little bit."

"And that's funny to you?" Wes raises a brow.

"You were so hot and cold; I couldn't get a read on you to save my life. No pun intended." I wink despite being unsure if he can see it. "Now it's like the floodgates have been opened and you're kissing my boo-boos and actually telling me how you feel."

"I guess I don't have anything to lose at this point... other than you."

And what do I have to lose?

Him. Dash. Bo.

I've already lost everything else that mattered to me —stripped away in the blink of an eye when my cunt of a boss decided to turn on me.

"What are we going to do?" I grip his hand tighter.

"The same thing we always do." He stares me directly in the eyes.

I finish his train of thought, "Survive."

Wes nods. "We need some time to heal, garner our strength."

The lights shut off without warning, everything going pitch black. I struggle to see through the darkness but keep my hold on Wes.

"I'm still here," he reassures me.

"There's a girl," I whisper. "In the cell next to me. She seems nice. She gave me a warning when they were turning the lights back on." I leave out the part where I was having phantom pains for no fucking reason.

Wes shifts a bit closer. "How did she know?"

"A guard." I keep my voice as quiet as I can.

"I think I met him." Wes lays on his side fully and rests my hand on his cheek. He brushes his lips against my skin again, sending a spike of pleasure up my arm, comforting me in the slightest. "Tell me about this girl."

I swallow and consider the promise I made her, and the one my soul had already made with Wes. Whether I acknowledge it or not, the connection he and I have runs both ways. I knew it from that first moment of seeing him, when that fluttering sensation had rattled in my chest and caused me to falter. I should have wiped that warehouse clean and killed every demon in there, but instead, I let that moment distract me and set my life on an entirely new course.

I settle on the things that I can confide in him without betraying the girl. "She was nice."

"You mentioned that already."

"She sounded young, maybe a few years younger

than me. Alluded that she had been here for a while. We didn't really talk much, but she told me there's no pattern to when they turn the lights on and off, and that they do it to fuck with us. It's easy to get disoriented when you lose track of the time. One minute they were off, and the next she urged me to shut my eyes, and a split second later, they were on."

Wes's body stiffens. "Was her name Jade?"

"No." Who's Jade? One of the people they were coming here to rescue? A previous lover? A family member? A friend?

He relaxes. "Oh."

But I don't ask him any of the questions that float into my mind, not when I'm afraid to know the answers to them. The thought of him belonging to anyone else weirdly unsettles my core. I've never been one for jealousy—the possessiveness feeling unfamiliar as it takes hold.

I avoid my train of thought. "What about you? Is there another cell on the other side?"

"Yes, but I'm not sure who's in it, or if there is anyone at all. They haven't made contact." He pauses and adds, "I can't imagine this is the most social of places."

"Will you distract me?" I mutter. Between the awkward position I'm in, both physically in this cage and overall in my life, and the countless other worries running through my head, I could use the tiny break.

"Are you in pain?" Wes repositions himself toward me.

"No."

He doesn't question my intentions anymore, instead, he asks something else. "What's your favorite color?"

A smile creeps across my face. "Red, what about you?"

"Blue, definitely blue. Like the sky, before our world turned to complete shit. Your eyes, that exact shade." His voice cracks a little. "What kind of red?"

I hadn't really put too much thought into it when he asked. Red was sort of a knee-jerk reaction to the inquiry. But now, I can't help imagining the glow of his irises, the flickers of flames that dance across his skin, the heat from his body and the inferno that engulfs him. I'm not entirely sure if red has always been my favorite, or if I had finally seen the color for all that it was when I witnessed him embody it. How do I articulate that though, without sounding like a fucking crazy person? And how do I choose just one when he is all of them? "Every variation, really," I finally say. To avoid any further probing, I initiate another round with him. "What's your biggest pet peeve?"

Wes exhales before answering. "Bo."

I let out a soft chuckle. "Mine, too."

"No, really, everything he does irritates me. The way he chews, his arrogant attitude, even how he sleeps. Have you heard him snore?"

"Can't say I've had the privilege."

"I don't recommend it. It'll keep you up all night." Wes presses his lips to my hand, almost like a habit he doesn't even realize he's formed.

What once would have repulsed me is a sensation I can't get enough of.

"Why keep him around then? If you dislike him so much."

"He's family." A solemn tone settles in his voice and despite not being able to see his face, I can picture the seriousness of his expression. "Both Wes and Dash."

"I never knew your kind could be so sentimental." A total truth at hearing his admission.

"There's a lot you don't know about us. That your kind refuses to acknowledge in their attempt to justify the eradication."

Nearly no time has passed since I made the life-altering mistake back at that warehouse, and already I've recognized the brutal reality that I've been conditioned to hate something I know next to nothing about. I should have died that day, but instead of meeting a cruel fate at the hands of three ruthless beings, I was tended to and nursed back to life. Part of me understands why Wes did it, due to the primal bond we share, but what did Dash or Bo have to gain from showing me kindness?

That alone is the first major wake-up call beating me over the head and planting little seeds of doubt in literally everything I believe in.

Add in the fact that each of them possesses a rare power that is unheard of in our realm, and you've already got a recipe for *what the fuck is going on.*

"Tell me more, then? I want to know everything." Because how else will I make sense of any of this without the facts.

"I will, I promise. Just not in here."

Not when it's unclear who might be listening in on our conversation. It's possible that we truly are alone, but risking any crucial details would be careless.

"We've probably already said too much," Wes says the words quietly in his attempt to shield them from prying ears.

"Will you keep talking? For a little bit? Doesn't have to be about anything in particular." The simple cadence of his voice is a salve to my aching soul.

"What's the most embarrassing thing you've ever done?"

"So, we're back to this game?" I grin and let my eyes close as I try to get more comfortable.

"I figure if I'm going to profess my love for you, the least we could do is get to know each other first." Wes kisses my hand again.

"And what better time than now."

"Mmhm."

I draw in a breath, ignoring the random spikes of pain throughout my battered body, and recall a memory to share. "Back when I was still in training, I was once woken up in the middle of the night to a simulation. I ran out and made the quickest time of all the recruits."

"I don't exactly see what's embarrassing about that. If anything, after watching you fight, I'm not at all surprised."

"I—um...I was naked."

Wes laughs faintly. "Wow, okay, yeah, I get it now."

"It was mortifying. My superiors were there overseeing the examination. My peers laughed and ended up being reprimanded, which made them even angrier at me. Originally for beating them, but beating them nude, and then them being docked points for finding the humor in it. Only made the whole *fitting-in* thing that much more difficult."

"Fitting in is overrated."

"Says the guy with two best friends. Growing up was lonely."

"I'm sorry; I didn't mean it like that." As if recalling a memory of his own, his tone softens, "I know what it's like being alone."

"What about you? What's your embarrassing tale?" I ask because I'd do anything to shift the direction of this conversation.

"Well," he says, considering his response. "It doesn't involve me being naked."

I shake my head and wait for him to continue.

"Do you speak Bravlavian?"

"Not fluently, no. Only a few words. Why?"

"I was once in a tavern predominantly filled with

Bravlav's. Hell, even the barkeep was. And as any respectable patron would do, I tried to adapt to their language since I was under the impression I had picked up enough over the years. Seemed like a considerate thing. Anyway, I went to the bar the same way I always do and ordered a pitcher of ale for the table. It wasn't until everyone within an earshot distance around me came to an abrupt silence, followed by Bo clasping onto my shoulders, nearly dying from laughter, that I realized something must have been lost in translation. Apparently, instead of asking for a pitcher of ale, I requested a bucket of semen."

A laugh bubbles out of my own chest and I take my free hand to clasp it over my mouth to suppress the noise. "Okay," I muster through the giggles. "You might have beaten me on this one." Just the very idea of Wes, a fierce whatever he is, stone-faced serious and asking some man for something so absurd is enough to make me temporarily forget my worries.

"Talk about mortifying," he resumes. "I felt like such an idiot. And the guys didn't let me live that one down for months. They still bring it up from time to time just to fuck with me."

"I can't say I blame them." I inch closer to the wall separating us and reposition the weight of my body pressing down on my shoulder. It's not much relief, but enough to keep my arm from falling completely asleep.

"Great, now you won't let me forget it either."

"Never," I tell him playfully. "My turn to ask a question."

"After that one, I don't know how much more I'm willing to share." Wes runs the tip of his nose along the side of my hand.

"If you could travel anywhere, where would you go?"

"Easy, Arthlia."

His response is strangely unexpected, and it takes me a moment to process he's even said it at all.

"You'd want to go to Earth? With the humans?"

"There are magical beings there, too," he tells me. "I've heard it's peaceful, nothing like what we face in this wretched realm."

I've never considered the alternative of living or even existing in any place other than my homeland. I've always fought to protect it and have done everything I could to make it better, safer. But what if my efforts have all been wasted? What if it was all for nothing? I've only further caused more of a divide, and I'm not sure today is any different than before I was even born. What's the point in fighting a war that will never be won? Especially when I doubt the side I'm on.

But with that startling realization, I grow aware that nothing is ever really what it seems. And the Earth realm could be just as dangerous as here in Prania. Monsters come in many shapes and sizes and some hide as people you may trust; authority figures you've looked up to your whole life. A month ago, I thought the demons were the only monsters plaguing this dimension, but now I find myself wanting to fight for them, not against them.

And on the off chance that what Wes is saying is true, our realm was sealed off decades ago, and travel to another is literally impossible.

For the sake of Wes's morale, I choose to go along with him anyway. "Sounds lovely."

For a split moment, possibilities linger between us, perhaps even a little hope that maybe one day we can escape from this nightmare. But dreams are simply that, flickering and temporary and always just out of grasp.

I'm reminded of that when the sound of metal scrapes against the stone floor. The door to Wes's chamber opens and there isn't a damn thing I can do about it.

In the time it takes me to blink, Wes is ripped away from me. My fingers claw desperately at the stale air filling the space where he once was. I strain to reach further through the small, grated section between our cells, and my flesh tears a bit more with each labored movement.

"Stop!" I yell out, but it's no use.

He's gone.

5
WREN

It's bizarre to care about someone else. Not to mention that very someone being the enemy. A monster I was told to fear. A demon I was instructed to kill.

I've always been on my own. And that's been okay. I've had ambitions. I've had goals and tasks and targets to eliminate. I was busy doing what I thought was right. Too distracted by my thirst for revenge to ever consider allowing feelings to develop. My entire life I've felt like an outsider in almost every situation. So, I took it upon myself to simply become the best. If I was going to be alone, at least I would be known for something.

I trained. I fought. I advanced my skills at every chance that presented itself.

I never questioned what I was doing or why I was doing it. My mother was killed by the vile creatures I was ordered to eliminate. That was as much proof as I needed to validate my actions.

But with each passing second of Wes being gone, and Dash and Bo out there on their own, no doubt struggling to stay alive, I'm reminded of just how very wrong I might have been.

I wince as another phantom pain strikes my chest; a rippling over my back like a whip slicing through my skin. I press my fingers to my shoulder expecting there to be blood and a gaping wound. But neither are there. The injuries are not my own despite sharing the agony.

"Are you okay?" A delicate voice whispers through the space between our rooms.

"Mmhm," I mutter through clenched teeth.

I'm no stranger to violence, but this is an entirely new experience.

"What's happening to you?" she asks me.

"I...I don't know." Is this some kind of magical abuse? A fresh take on torturing I've never heard of in all my years? What else are these sadists doing within the walls of this prison? And for what possible gain?

"You should try to get some sleep," Franny suggests.

"Has this ever happened to you?" I lean my head against the barrier between us and let the weight of my body fall into it.

"No." She lets out a breath. "Although, this place has no shortage of tricks up its sleeve."

"I just hope he's okay." The words leave my mouth before I can catch them. I don't mean to say this out loud, but my worries have transformed into something I can barely maintain.

Between the poor conditions, the injuries, and the heaviness of the entire situation, I find my mind slipping in a way that I never could have imagined. I thought I was stronger than this. More capable. I've been through extreme situations numerous times but for once it's not just me on the line, and that hurts in a way that no physical pain can.

My thoughts go wild at the possibilities. The endless things that could happen to these three men who put their trust in me. I marched them to their demise. And now they're trapped because of me. Dash and Bo might as well be locked in cells here with us considering they have no way of escaping hunter territory without someone on the inside helping them out. If I was a betting woman, I'd wager the likelihood of them finding a demon sympathizer slim to none.

Franny shuffles from her spot on the other side of the wall. "If it's any consolation, it's rare they actually kill anyone."

I consider her words, allow them to be processed, then analyze them again. I blink through the yellow light in my cell, my gaze darting to and from, but not really settling on any one thing in particular.

"What do you mean?" I ask her. "How can you be so sure?"

"I told you, I've been here for a while, as have a lot

of others." She hesitates before adding, "I can *sense* when death is near."

I swallow the realization of what she is. "You're a…" But I don't finish my statement because she and I already know.

She's a banshee.

Another rarity in our world. A female who can sense impending demise. One whose screams can shatter glass and slice through a person like the sharpest of blades. A powerful and incredible creature who is often underestimated. Banshees are rumored to have descended from the fae and in some lore, are known to be immortal.

Two weeks ago, I would have killed her without thinking twice, but now, all I want to do is ask questions and learn more about her. I curse this situation, but without it, I'm not sure I ever would have woken up from the lifelong slumber I've been in—killing anything that smelled demonic.

That familiar scraping sound floats from Franny's cell into mine—her door being opened.

The guard steps closer into the room. "Making friends with a hunter, are we?"

"A hunter?" she blurts out.

Metal pings on the floor, followed by the door shutting.

My own door moves next, and the man drops a tray inside and kicks at it with his dirty boot. "Traitor," he slurs before disappearing behind the thing keeping me locked in here.

"It's not what you think," I tell my cellmate.

Franny sniffs in twice. "You smell like a demon, I don't understand."

I could lie, tell her that I am, and use Bo's mark as a way to maintain this unlikely alliance, but that would be deceitful and if she found out, there's no telling the damage it would do.

My gaze falls to the grayish-looking pile of sludge on the tray that was brought in. The cup of liquid tipped over on its side, the meager contents spilling onto the filthy floor. My stomach betrays me with a growl, and it's then that I realize how fucking parched I am. I struggle to swallow the sandpaper coating my tongue and focus on the wall. If I stand any chance of breaking out of this torture chamber, I can't lose the one alliance I was trying to build.

"I *was* a hunter, but I'm not anymore," I begin to explain.

She cuts me off, her voice coated in disappointment, "Once a hunter, always a hunter."

"Things have changed, *I've* changed." Despite my dehydration, unwanted tears fill my eyes.

I am not weak. I will not cry. I am stronger than this.

But how can I remain this gallant force when my entire life has been nothing but a lie?

I've taken lives—too many to count, and for what?

And now I'm having an internal existential crisis

when I should be pulling up my bootstraps and figuring out how to get out of this fucking mess.

No—I won't let this place break me—not like this.

So, I do the thing I probably shouldn't, tell her the truth. "I was marked by a demon."

"An alpha," she mutters.

"Yes," I confirm. "I'd be lying if I said we didn't start off as enemies, but it quickly became more than that. I..." Recalling the memory of that arrogant demon who pushed every one of my buttons, my heart constricts at the involuntary feelings that have developed. I never meant for it to grow into what it has, but as much as I try to deny that Bo and I share anything in common, we're actually more alike than we thought. And when you're taught to hate each other, the lack of bullshit pleasantries really shows you what kind of person someone is. It's almost like there's a mutual respect because you don't get a muddled-down version, you get the real them. Through that lack of false pretenses, I was able to see Bo more clearly.

"You're telling me you fell in love with a demon?" Franny drags the tray in her cell toward her.

"No," I blurt out. "It's not that."

"Mmhm, okay. You're falling for the enemy. Same thing."

I follow suit and bring the pathetic platter closer, careful not to spill the rest of the water even more. I tip the cup to my mouth and let a few drops fall onto my tongue. There's no telling if any of this is drugged, but starving to death isn't a great choice, either. I'll take my chances in an attempt to replenish my strength, at least for the time being. If only Wes could heal me with his words like he's done in the past, I'd snap the neck of the next person who walked into this room and free anyone I could on my way to freedom.

Another blast of pain strikes my back unexpectedly. I grit my teeth, exhaling through my nose, as I wait for another to come. Glancing toward the empty cell beside me, I worry about what Wes might be experiencing. I take small comfort in knowing that Franny hasn't anticipated an upcoming death, but things could change in the blink of an eye, the last couple of weeks of my life have proven exactly that.

"The alpha," Franny says between scraping some of her sludge into her mouth. "Is he your other cellmate?"

"No," I tell her.

"But you're worried about him, too?"

I breathe in deeply and consider her question and the hidden implications behind it. Do I care for the alpha? Of course. But do I also care for the infuriating man who shares a mate bond with me? Without a doubt. And then there's Dash, who surprised every one of us by dying and bursting into flames, only to be reborn again. My heart was torn to shreds when I thought he was gone—that I was responsible for his death. Not that it's any less true, but witnessing him come back to life was a second chance I never imagined I'd get with him.

From then on out, I've wanted to protect him, to prevent something like that from happening again, but here we are, me and Wes locked up with a one-way ticket to Hell, and Dash and Bo no doubt following suit at any given time.

Do I tell Franny all of that though? No, because what good would it do other than give out more vital information that I should probably keep tucked away. Still, she deserves some part of the truth. "Yes," I respond because there's no denying that I am worried about Wes.

"Interesting." She places her bowl onto her tray and pushes it across the floor. "You should eat while you can. Sometimes they come back in and take it before we get a chance."

"Thank you." I spoon some of the gross mixture into my mouth and swallow it without another thought.

"What for?"

"Choosing to still talk to me, to give me advice on how to survive in here."

Franny repositions herself on the other side of the wall. "I guess I would want someone to do the same for me." She hesitates before adding, "But that doesn't mean I trust you."

"Good," I reassure her. "Don't."

Franny chuckles, whatever she's about to say cut off by the creaking of the door to her cell opening.

"Up," a guy commands. "I said *up*, bitch."

I press my palm against the cold stone between us

and wish I could knock it down and punch the asshole who insulted her. "Don't fucking touch her!" I yell in their direction.

My words fall flat as the man gets his way. And now I'm left here, once again all alone, wondering when it'll be my turn to be taken.

"Wren," a deep but quiet voice calls out to me.

I blink my eyes open and rise from the dirt-covered concrete floor, dusting off my legs and tucking my hair behind my ears.

"Wren," they whisper to me again, only this time with haggard breaths. "I need you."

Is this another trick? A figment of my imagination? My mind finally losing it once and for all?

"Wes?" I tiptoe closer to the space he's been held captive in. "Are you okay?"

But instead of him responding, it's the man from a moment ago. "He needs your help."

There's something strange about the way the sound is coming more from my own head than in the other room. It doesn't quite make sense at all.

"Don't you hurt him," I tell whoever might be over there. A threat lingering on each word.

Silence fills the space and I hold my breath in anticipation of whatever comes next.

Finally, the melancholy man continues, "You're the only one who can save him."

"I..." An ache fills my chest. "I don't know how." The door to my room is sealed shut, and I have no doubt his is, too. And even if I *could* get through both barriers and fight off anyone who might try to stop me, I don't have healing powers.

"You must try."

His statement is followed by the sudden clank of metal being turned. The guard I expect to enter my room never comes. Instead, only the sound of my wild heart fills the air. I stare for a long moment at the thing keeping me locked in here. With cautious steps, I move toward it. My pulse thumps in my ears as I grow more uncertain of this entire situation. I place my hand carefully on the lever and hold my breath as it gives under my weight.

To my utter disbelief, the door creaks open.

A million different scenarios cross my mind, all of them ending in more questions than answers. A sinking in my gut tells me I have to get to him, that I must use this opportunity to do what the voice instructed me to. I'm not quite sure why I trust it so blindly, but I'm convinced it wouldn't steer me wrong.

Poking my head through the opening, I study the eerie hallway. Not a soul in sight—demon or guard. I creep further, the hair on my skin raising in anticipation of a threat I cannot determine just yet. I stay close to the interior wall and slink my body along the rough surface.

This is all too good to be true, and I'm damn well aware of that. My main priority is to get to Wes, beyond that I'll figure out after.

My breath catches when I spot the slight opening in his cell. I swallow down the mystery of who unlocked both of our chambers and file it in the *what the fuck is going on* folder for later.

My entire body tenses as I press my hand against the door and push it ajar enough for me to slip inside. A second passes before my eyes adjust, and when they do, my reaction is more urgent. The space seems to expand with each passing second it takes me to reach him.

Wes, collapsed in the corner of the room, blood coating his body.

"Oh no, no, no," I babble while dropping to my knees next to him. "Please be alive, don't be dead." I grip his face in my palms and tilt it toward me. Rubbing my thumbs on his cheeks, I silently pray to the gods, to the angels, to anyone who might be listening. *Please let him live.* He can't be dead. Not like this.

Each moment drags on and I'm reminded of watching Dash be killed right in front of me. The snap of his neck, the thud of his body hitting the ground, the pain ripping through my chest. The wound that was mended when Dash resurrected is now torn apart and gushing at the seams. I was lucky to get him back, but what if luck isn't on my side this time? What if when

Wes dies, that's it? What if he's gone from this world forever?

My stomach turns as nausea rises. I blink and a flash of my vision takes me back to when I was only a small child, ignorant to the dangers of the world. My dad was gone, fighting in a war that was impossible to win, and my mom was murdered as I cowered and hid from the monsters that took everything from me. They burned down my home and left me with nothing but a thirst for revenge that would never be satiated. I've spent the rest of my life trying to feed that hunger. To kill every single demon I could. But what if the things I think are monsters aren't the ones I should fear after all?

What if the true villains of this story are my own kind?

A flutter of hope returns as my fated mate's eyelids twitch, and finally part ways, gifting me with his life.

"Wren?" he struggles to speak.

"I'm here, I'm right here," I reassure him.

His blood speckled cheeks turn up slightly and he raises his arm toward my face. He rests his palm gently on my cheek. "You are, aren't you?"

"Wes," I breathe into him. "We have to go. I have to get you out of here." But before I can convince him further, the door I had left cracked open is shut, the metal jangling is an unfortunate indicator that we're now locked in place.

"Come here." Wes grips my waist and, despite his tattered exterior, manages to drag me onto his lap.

If we're going to be trapped in this hellhole, at least we're together.

"What did they do to you?" I ask him.

"Nothing I can't handle." Wes wraps his arms around me and holds me close. He rests his head in the crook of my neck.

I flinch when my own arms graze his back. I wiggle from his grasp to take a better look. The torn fabric from his shirt intermingles with the ripped flesh struggling to heal. The wounds cover the span of his trunk, some of them much deeper than the rest. A familiar sensation lingers along my own skin, a ghost of the phantom pain I had experienced earlier.

Is something like that even possible? Could I have been feeling what Wes was while they were torturing him? I've never heard of such a thing in all my life. But at this point, why would I be surprised that he and I would share that kind of bond?

"I'm fine, really." Wes steadies my shoulders and returns me to his lap.

"Wes." I fix my gaze on him. "I thought you were dead when I came in here."

His hard demeanor relaxes. "I was resting, that's all. I didn't mean to worry you."

"I can't wait until these cuffs are off and you can go back to not being able to lie to me."

"You noticed that, did you?" He smiles through his

pain until his brows furrow. "Wait, how did you get in here?" Wes tilts his head to look around me, toward the door.

This is the part where I could do the same, withhold the truth. But is that really the best course of action? Secrets will only no doubt get us killed. And if we're going to die, what's the point in keeping things from each other? The things that might make a difference in whether we live or die.

I choose to follow my gut. "I have to tell you something, but it's going to sound crazy."

"I'm sure it can't get any crazier than this." He motions into the space at nothing in particular.

"I...I heard a voice. It told me you needed help. I questioned it, but then the door to my cell unlocked, and when I went into the hall, no one was there. I came straight here, and your chamber was open, too. That's when I saw you lying there." My voice trails off with the memory of his seemingly lifeless body.

"Hey." He tips my chin up and stares into my eyes. That usual glowing red is replaced with a dull crimson, another reminder of how much they've stolen from him here. "I'm sorry you thought I was dead, but I'm not, okay? That must have been triggering for you. I'll do my best to appear more alive from here on out."

I sigh and shake my head. Even in such terrible circumstances, he's able to soften my resolve. "Is it supposed to feel like this?"

"What?" He tucks my wild hair behind my ear.

"A fated bond."

Wes swallows and stiffens slightly. "Don't worry about all that."

I narrow my gaze. "I'm as in this as you are, buddy."

"Buddy?" he laughs. "Don't be concerned about the bond, Wren. That's between me and my hound. It shouldn't affect you in any way...other than both of us being a little possessive over you." Wes tugs me closer. "Or maybe a lot—we can't exactly control it."

"And you think I can?" I bite at my bottom lip.

At this very subtle movement, the atmosphere shifts and desire swirls around us.

"What are you saying?" Wes eyes my mouth briefly.

"It's not only you, *or* your hound, Wes."

"That's impossible."

"It's safe to say this world has proven anything is possible. That I'm just as much your fated mate, as you are mine." I have to prove it to him, to get him to understand. "I could feel when they were hurting you. Those marks on your back, the strikes across your face. I felt that, too. What else would possibly explain that?"

He opens his mouth, but I cut him off.

"That voice I heard, the one telling me to come to you. That I had to save you. It took me until now to realize it, but...Wes...I think it was your hound. You said you haven't heard from him, but what if whatever ties us together allows for that contact? There's no way that would be possible if this were only one-sided. You have to believe that."

His dull eyes glisten with all the things still unspoken between us. "Wren, I…" He cups both of my cheeks in his hands, the span of them encompassing nearly my whole face. "I really want to kiss you right now."

"What's stopping you?"

And after what could have been a lifetime ago since the two touched, he presses his warm lips against mine, our mouths desperate to reconnect with one another and confirm the truth of this link.

I move, either by his hands that guide me, or by the natural manner in which my body pleads to be closer to him. The reasoning doesn't matter. My main concern is discovering the shape we make together. Straddling his waist, his growing erection presses into my bottom.

Wes swirls his tongue over mine and lets out an animalistic but suppressed moan.

I allow him to deepen the kiss and grind myself on top of him. I ache in an entirely different way than I did an hour ago. Every bit of pain and suffering is replaced with the longing I have for him. Should we be discussing a way out of here? Probably. But with the likelihood of us both dying being so fucking high, why not enjoy ourselves a little while we have the chance?

He breaks away and trails his lips down my chin and onto the base of my neck, over my collarbone. "Wren, we…"

Pleasure cascades over me at his touch—a pure heaven while trapped here in this hell.

Digging my fingers into his hair, I moan and tilt my head for him to get a better angle. I wrench at my armored top and wish for the first time in my life that it weren't in the way between a demon and my skin. Finally, I pull it to the side and expose part of my chest to him.

He immediately takes my breast into his hand, massaging it and teasing my nipple with his teeth. I nearly explode from the contact and the ever-rising urge to feel him inside of me. The craving shifts from a want to a need and consumes my every thought.

With my hand still twirled through his luscious locks, and a carnal desperation to taste him on my tongue, I yank him away with the intent of kissing him again. I expect to find his drab gaze, but instead, I'm met with the simmering glow of that recognizable red.

"Wes," I mutter while the revelation courses through me.

His hound side reacting to us being together means that maybe we might actually make it out of here alive.

But before I can tell him that, ice-cold water is thrown onto my face.

When I open my eyes, I'm not with Wes at all, not even in his room. I'm in mine, laying in the corner up against the wall, a guard standing above me with an empty bucket.

"Wake up, bitch." The man kicks my leg and then reaches down, gripping me by the collar and yanking me onto my feet.

"Don't fucking touch me," I spit at him.

He wastes no time in reacting, taking his pail and slamming it into my face.

The room spins but I regain my footing. My blood splatters onto the floor and the man's shoes.

"Great, now I'm contaminated."

I glare up at the tall and stocky older man. There's nothing special about him. Not his standard-issue hair-cut, clothing, or the privileged arrogance seeping from every inch of him.

What a fucking waste of oxygen.

I damn well know I shouldn't, but fueled by my rage to put this man in his place, I suck in a breath and spit the blood that had pooled in my mouth onto his ugly face.

I smile as he turns red, both from his own anger and my generous decoration.

His attention momentarily flashes behind me and alerts me of a newcomer to our little party.

I duck and spin, avoiding the man who entered the space, but what I didn't expect was the third asshole jabbing me with a fucking cattle prod.

The jolt drops me to my knees, placing me right in the way of the first guy's fist.

What a bunch of cowards needing three of them to take down *one* girl.

I brace myself and wipe at my nose, pushing off the floor and searing my gaze at each of them. "Is that all you fucking got?" I spit onto the bucket guy's shoes again, making sure to really leave a mark.

"When we get done with you, you're going to wish you were fucking dead."

That threat is the last thing I hear before the man with the prod reels up his leg and kicks me square in the chest. I slam into the hard wall behind me, and my entire world turns black.

6

DASH

It would be really cool if my only superpower wasn't dying.

I mean, what the heck am I supposed to do with that? Die? How does that help anyone? I guess that means there's less risk. So, I can be the one going head first into danger, because if I do die, I'll just come back to life. But when literally everyone else has *supernatural* abilities, dying over and over again seems kind of pointless. It's not like I can *die* someone to death.

I'm sort of an okay fighter, and demons really love to underestimate my ability to fend for myself. I can't say I blame them though. I'm puny compared to them. In their eyes, I'm a pathetic human trying to blend into a world where I don't belong. On occasion, I'm able to kick a little ass and stay alive.

Luckily, Bo and Wes, two incredibly powerful creatures, took me under their metaphorical wings. Although, I wouldn't be surprised if either one of them sprouted the feather-covered things and took off into flight, considering this entire realm continues to amaze me.

Despite what everyone thinks of demons, they've had my back from day one, and I've never questioned that. But now, now one of them has been taken hostage, along with a woman I'm falling for at the light of speed. Damn it, the light of speed. No! SPEED OF LIGHT.

GET IT TOGETHER, DASH.

Every time I think of her my brain turns to mush. My palms get all sweaty, and my heart races. Partly because of how freaking lucky I am that she gave me the time of day, but mostly because I'm concerned that I'll never see her again. And unlike me, Wren is not a phoenix. If she dies, she's gone for good, and I'm not sure there's a world I ever want to live in without her.

I know what you're thinking—heck, I'm thinking it myself. Something along the lines of, "Whoa there, slow down, man. You've only just met the female."

But, Wren? She's not your average lady. No, she's fire and ice, sweet and savory, and brains and brawn, all mixed up into one. She's fierce, brave, and stubborn-headed as all get out, but there's this unspoken passion behind everything she does. Foolish, most definitely, but her tenacity is inspiring, and I cannot help but be drawn to how damn captivating she is. For the first time since I woke up in this realm with no recollection of who I am—I feel alive. I feel seen.

"Are you talking to yourself?" Bo smacks my shoulder and continues on his path through these thickly covered woods.

"Don't you?"

He turns toward me, raising a brow and then focusing forward again. "You fucking with me?"

"Probably." Maybe I should take a chapter out of Bo's book and disassociate from my thoughts and feelings until they bubble up into an uncontrollable rage.

Seems like a total dude thing to do.

I'll pass.

"Where are we going, anyway?" I ask him.

We've been on the move for days now, crisscrossing and zig-zagging our path in every kind of direction, not going the same way twice out of fear that our scent might get picked up and followed. And on the chance that it does, the erratic pattern will hopefully send them on a wild goose chase.

Our supplies are dwindling fast and if we don't find a way to replenish them soon, Bo's hunger will no doubt get the best of him. Which isn't saying much because that man prides himself in being as bad as possible.

"I can smell some hunters up ahead." Bo points his long arm in front of him.

I reach out and latch onto his shoulder. "Hey."

He yanks free of my grasp but pauses. "What?"

"I have a serious question." I'm not sure why it never dawned on me until now.

Bo sighs and rolls his eyes. "No, Dash, I'm not attracted to you."

I narrow my gaze at him and chuckle. "Okay for one, I don't buy that. And for two, that's not what I was going to ask. But you're going to think it's weird, so hear me out."

Bo crosses his arms over his chest and waits for me to continue. "Fine," he huffs out. "What is it?" He takes a few cautious peeks in the direction we were heading and then behind him.

"Can you smell me?" I stare at him and motion toward my body.

"I'm going to stab you."

"You said you would listen."

"I can listen and stab at the same time."

"Seriously, Bo, smell me. What do I smell like?"

"Stop saying the word 'smell' so much. *That* is weird."

I pull the blade from its sheathed spot in my waistband. "Fine, my turn. Now I'm the one going to do the stabbing."

Bo laughs but remains arms crossed. "What're you going to do with that thing? Tease me with a good time?"

I grip the handle and swipe it in the air between us, rustling the hair spilling onto his shoulder.

He narrows his gaze and bobs his head up and down. "Okay then, this could get fun."

But when I move the knife the next time, he reaches out, and in a split second, he's disarmed me and turned the blade around to point it at my chest. "You might be a phoenix, Dash, but that doesn't mean I won't kill you."

"Fine, whatever. Do I *smell* like a phoenix though?" I wiggle under his grasp. "Let go of me, you buffoon."

He complies, flipping the knife around to hold it by the sharp end and give it back to me. "No, dumbass. You don't *smell* like a phoenix. What's this all about?"

"It was something you said. You can smell the hunters. And they can smell you, right?"

"I swear to my maker, if you say smell one more time." Bo rubs his temple and exhales dramatically.

"This conversation would be over a heck of a lot quicker if you would cooperate."

Bo glances around us, always on alert for a potential threat. He's much better at this survival thing than I am. "You are correct. I guess you could say we have a natural scent. Them and us. And it is detectable to the trained tracker, yes. Most hunters are skilled at it, like it's part of their training protocol. Most demons are too stupid to sharpen theirs. And now that I've answered you, care to tell me why you're asking about something I assumed you already knew?"

"I did, but hear me out. I don't have a scent either way."

"I'm still missing your point. Can you just spell it out already so we can get this show on the road?" Bo extends his arm and uses the other to pull it in a deep stretch in front of his chest while he waits on me to continue.

"I can sneak in undetected," I say confidently.

Bo stops moving. "Where?"

I point to where we were heading. "Food, big guy."

He scrunches up his face like he's deep in thought. "I don't know, man. This is probably where Wes would tell us it's not worth the risk and come up with some other plan."

I widen my eyes and peer into the empty space around us. "But Wes isn't here. And considering the position he's currently in, perhaps we should reassess who's the boss around here."

Bo scoffs. "He isn't *the boss*."

"Is too, you basically just said it yourself."

"We're a team. That's much different than there being *one* leader. Just because I consider his input doesn't mean he's the top dog."

I let out a chuckle. "I see what you did there."

"Besides, you know damn well Wren will have my ass for putting your life in danger any more than it already is." Bo rifles through his bag to come up empty. Through the silence of the eerie forest around us, I can make out the grumble of his belly.

"I think your stomach speaks for both of us."

He tosses the bag over his shoulder and starts

walking away from me. "It's your funeral," he quietly calls back.

"Aw, I'll never get one of those." I take off after him.

Bo shoves me playfully. "Don't tempt me, I'll get creative enough to find a way for you to permanently die."

The rest of the walk is quiet, aside from the dirt giving way under our tired feet and the occasional branch falling in the distance. It isn't until we're nearly upon the hunters that the tune of their voices begins to carry toward us.

Bo gets us as close as possible without drawing unwanted attention and allows us to remain concealed.

We huddle behind a large tree surrounded by lush shrubbery and assess the situation.

Three buildings fill the space, and a few bodies walk to and from. Nothing major, but considering we're trapped in enemy territory, we cannot afford to have this many hunters aware of our whereabouts.

It's equal parts shocking and strange that we haven't already been found and captured, thrown into the hell Wren and Wes have gotten themselves wrapped up in. Word of us hasn't traveled the way I assumed it would, which only raises more questions. Why would they be keeping that a secret?

"That one," Bo points to the building on the far left. "That's where they're eating." He hovers his finger to the other end. "That looks like their lodging."

"What's the one across the way?" I whisper.

"Supplies, I'm guessing. Maybe an infirmary." Bo side-eyes me. "Food and water are our priority. Don't get any ideas."

"Me? I didn't say anything. I was just curious." I might be a phoenix who can resurrect, but I can still get injured. As can a certain woman we're all pining after. It wouldn't hurt to grab some of that stuff on the off chance we figure out a way to free her from Rock Bridge.

"Wes can heal Birdie."

I crane my neck to look at him. "Who's the weird one now? Stop reading my mind."

"I'm not. You just have a terrible poker face."

"What's poker?"

"I sometimes forget you were born not too long ago. It's a card game, requires strategy and a hefty dose of luck."

"Teach me sometime?"

"Sure." He slaps my shoulder in a way that makes me think he's only trying to shut me up. "I guess we have forever now that you're never-ending and all."

I take a deep breath. "Is that the case? I don't know anything about being a phoenix. I get unlimited lives?"

"Uh, maybe that's a question for someone else. How about you try not to die in the meantime."

"Deal." I focus on the hunters up ahead. "Wait, you're immortal?"

Bo nods stiffly. "Something like that."

"Hmph. Cool. What about Wes?"

"Wes is sort of an enigma." He shrugs.

But where does that leave Wren in the mix of all of this? Will there be a day when no amount of safety precautions can erase the natural progression of her life? I'm destined to just continue living for...ever? It's no wonder I have no family—they're probably all dead.

"If I get any closer, they'll be able to pick up my scent." Bo pulls a knife from seemingly out of nowhere. "Here, it's smaller than yours; easier to handle in close quarters. And if you need to cut anything, it has a wickedly sharp blade."

"Thanks," I tell him while taking the thing into my own hand. "It'll be fine, this will be easy. Don't worry about me."

"You reassuring yourself or me?" Bo steadies my shoulders and looks me square in the eye. "I'll be watching you the whole time, and I refuse to let you have all the fun if shit goes down."

My cheek turns up into a grin. "Mmhm. That's an awfully weird way of saying you care about me."

His gaze falls to the knife he handed me. "It's not too late for me to stab you."

"You're sweet, Bo, really. Such a softie." I pat his arm and step around him to find the path to the hunters.

Steadying my breath, I walk further away from the last being who was protecting me in this dangerous world. I glance back once to find that I can no longer spot him. A chill flutters up my spine. I've done risky shit before, and we've been apart in the past, but never when I've been marching headfirst into enemy territory with no chance of escaping. We're quite literally trapped in this secured portion of our world and the only person who can save us is trapped in an impenetrable prison. I'd live forever on the run like this if it meant she stayed alive, though. Only, there's no way of guaranteeing that—so the only thing me and Bo can do now is survive and then try to find a way to free her, to free Wes.

The ground crunches softly beneath my boots, a much-contrasted sound to that of my thudding heart. I scan the near vicinity, pretending like I'm Bo, and try to identify any potential threats. The few hunters walking to and from seem to be so consumed in their own missions that they don't even give much attention to each other, let alone me.

The rear of this mess hall gets closer and closer with every step I take toward it—the reality of this plan succeeding grows more likely by the moment. My chest warms with the possibility that maybe we aren't so screwed after all.

If it were Bo stalking into this camp, he'd be outed prior to anyone latching their sights on him. His scent is strong and powerful, at least that's what I'm told. He smells like musk and rain to me. He could use a wash more often than he settles on, but it's not a *demonic* scent. Me, on the other hand, I'm able to walk in undetected, which means we might finally have found our advantage.

I approach the mound of crates stacked near the building and quickly release my pack from over my shoulder. Popping the top on one of them, I'm assaulted in the best way ever by the aroma of bread. My cheek turns up into a grin knowing how happy this will make Bo, and the realization that maybe we won't starve to death out here. Oh, how fun would that be, dying over and over painfully and terribly.

I shove a few loaves into my bag and put the lid back in place. The less it looks like I was here, the better. I pry another off and revel at the sight of bright red apples. I waste no time placing some of them next to the commandeered bread. Moving onto another crate, I peer to check my surroundings. My heart races with the excitement and terror of this entire situation. My next discovery is lined with various meats, mostly that of the dried variety. My stomach grumbles its approval. I put the top on and decide to risk it by taking the whole thing.

Gripping the sides of the box, I stand and do my best to hide the triumphant emotions bubbling to the surface. If I can get out of here without getting caught, Bo and I will be eating good tonight, and for the foreseeable future. Maybe hope isn't as lost as we once thought it was.

I could kick myself in the ass for my optimism when the door to the back of the building flies open, and a man steps through it. The thing latches shut behind him, leaving the two of us out here alone.

"What are you doing?" His serious tone ripples through me.

His posture is stiff and rugged; his frame is easily a few inches taller than mine. The man is bigger, but the softness leads me to think it's not all muscle behind his clothing.

Don't panic, Dash, don't panic.

I swallow the immediate fear that consumes my entire body. "Following orders, sir."

The man raises a brow, assessing whether he should believe my cover story. His nostrils flare slightly, perhaps determining if I am friend or foe.

This is it, the moment my entire hasty plan falls apart. Endless possibilities run through my mind, all of them ending in my demise. At least Bo won't be slowed down by my dead weight—the only silver lining I can come up with while this man takes a freaking eternity to decide his next move.

He steps forward and I brace myself for impact. I'd reach for my knife, but that would be too obvious, too foolish at this point. I'd draw attention to our direction and that would only put Bo more at risk of being caught. The only way to give him a fighting chance of getting away will be to cause as little commotion as possible.

"Take this to B11." The guy plops the package in his grasp on top of the box I'm holding in my arms. The one

I hadn't even noticed he was holding in the sheer terror of him appearing in front of me. "And when you're done." He nods toward the other building near us. "They could use another hand cleaning the weapons."

I unclench my jaw and tip my head in agreement, hoping the sweat trickling down my back doesn't spread to my face. "Yes, sir. Anything else, sir?" Because compliance very well could be the best course of action right now.

He lets my request linger between us for what feels like an eternity, causing me to second guess saying it. "No, that'll be all." He points to the package in my possession. "Make sure that gets to B11, son." He rotates to walk back in the direction he came.

"Sir?" I find myself saying.

He turns on his heel and waits for me to continue.

"I seem to have misplaced my canteen. Do you know where I can find a replacement?"

The stout man sighs and glances down at his side, pausing for a second before making an internal decision. He unlatches his own from the hook on his waistband. "Here. Do yourself a favor and try not to lose this one. *Others* won't be as kind as I am."

I reach out awkwardly from underneath the boxes in my arms, and take the thing from him, noting the weight of the liquid inside sloshing around.

Good, it's nearly full.

"Thank you, sir," I tell him as he nods stiffly and goes on his way.

I exhale slowly and blink down at the crates left untouched. I could gather more, give us a better chance of survival, but if I linger any longer, I'm only increasing the likelihood that I get caught. And what good will this risky mission have been if I fuck up like that? I must be smarter, more strategic, and get back with Bo sooner rather than later. I've already pushed my luck enough by interacting with this hunter.

When I'm positive the man is on the other side of the door he came from, I step away from the treasure. With my arms full of goods, I tiptoe and glance behind me, making a beeline for the forest-covered area Bo is hiding out in. If I can make it to the covered area, I can breathe easy knowing I secured provisions for us to get by.

Each step closer feels like another that I'm cheating death. I wait for someone to come and stop me, but it never happens. Inching nearer to the finish line, I grow more satisfied that my plan is working. I had my doubts, that's for sure, but something crazy had to be done if we stand any chance of living through this nightmare. What good are we to Wren and Wes if we wither away out here?

I cross over the thickly covered barrier shielding us from the prying eyes of the hunters at the camp below. I exhale and blink my vision clear as it adjusts to the dimmer light of the concealment. Pausing, I skim my surroundings, and wait for the broody and arrogant demon friend of mine to appear. I guess we hadn't talked this all the way through, but I sort of assumed he would greet me upon my arrival. I ignore the sinking pit in my gut and chalk it up to residual anxiety from my foolish scheme.

Continuing to move through the woods, I focus intently on the sounds of the area. It's not until I climb a little further that my vision confirms my fear before my hearing.

Bo, unmoving, lifeless on the ground. Shackles on his wrist, and a dagger pointed at him.

"Oh, it's just another hunter." The one man says to the other.

I drop the boxes and let the straps of my backpack slide over my shoulders and down my arms. The bag hits the ground with a thud, and apples roll out in the wake of the fall. I'm not even sure of the movements I make, but I find the knife Bo had given me gripped tightly in my hand.

Still thinking I'm on his side, the man holding the blade against Bo's throat smiles. "You want in on this, too?"

I don't say a word, I only continue to step toward this disturbing sight. Rage builds within me and over-powers my ability to function; instead, it takes control of my arm, raising it up, my opposite fist grabbing onto the hair on the man's head firmly to secure him in place as I drive the cold metal into his chest.

Wide-eyed and mouth gaped, the realization finally settles in. Blood overflows from his lips and he struggles to breathe through the liquid no doubt pooling in his lungs.

"What the fuck!" the other guy calls out.

I let the man in my grasp fall to the ground and slide the crimson-stained blade free of his torso. I allow the rage to guide me, to take the reins and steer me through.

I'm met with a blow to the face, throwing me off balance and onto all fours. I spit my own blood onto the dirt and glare up at the man who was planning to kill Bo. I've fought countless demons in the past, but only rarely a hunter. Their skills far surpass mine, but at least I don't have to worry about magic I cannot anticipate.

The guy acts irrationally, literally throwing himself toward me with his knife clasped in his hands.

I roll out of the way and laugh as he falls to the ground.

"What are you? A fucking sympathizer?" He regains himself while I do the same.

We both climb to our feet and face one another.

"You're scum, that's for sure." He spits onto the ground between us.

Are his words supposed to intimidate me? If anything, they only continue to fuel the metaphorical fire raging from within.

I don't reply, I only wait for him to strike. To make a mistake so I can end his life just like I did to his friend.

He does exactly what I expect, advances in haste.

I duck and slice my own blade at him, cutting through a thin layer of his pants. I repeat the motion back and forth rapidly and finally draw a bit of blood.

The man, about equal to my size, curses and stumbles back, his free hand reaching toward the new wounds on his shins. I use the opportunity to swipe at the dirt-covered ground and toss the debris into his face.

His palms go to cover his eyes but it's too late, the dust causes him to temporarily lose his vision.

I grin and advance on him in his moment of weakness, my knife gripped in my fist and the blade aimed at his heart.

Only, somehow, this man isn't as incapacitated as one would assume. The loss of his vision almost makes him more aware of his surroundings. His body pivots toward me and at the moment I'm about to strike him, he jumps out of the way. My own form stumbles from the misjudged target, and is met by a blow across the back, knocking the wind from my chest and my legs out from under me.

Shit.

I hit the ground hard, my hands desperate to absorb the impact and protect the rest of my body. The flesh on my palm stings, a painful reminder of what is at stake here. My life. Bo's life. And ultimately, the lives of Wren and Wes.

"What are you, anyway?" The man calls out from behind me. He sniffs the air aggressively. "His scent is strong, pungent...I get nothing on you." He kicks me square in the side and flips me onto my back.

I blink through the automatic tears that form in my eyes and frantically search for the knife that was lost in the fall. My fingers dig into the ground, scanning the surface all around me for any clue on where it might be.

In a flash, he climbs on top of me, straddling my waist and pinning me to the ground. His fist meets my jaw in a blast of pain that sends sparkling things dancing in my vision. He hits me again, and again, my face reacting immediately to the impact and swelling.

I do my best to block his blows, yet still, most of them are effective.

I buck but it's no use, I cannot dismount him for the life of me.

It's only a matter of time until he finishes me off and then returns to Bo to complete the slaughter. All of this because I was too weak to overpower a hunter. All of this because I am useless in this world.

The man strikes me once more.

A new fear rises within me. Not that of being killed, but of my phoenix powers activating after my death. I'll resurrect to find Bo murdered and there not being a damn thing I can do about it. He'll be dead and it'll be my fault.

A burst of renewed spirit and hope explodes inside of me when my fingers graze the cold surface of what I pray is my knife. I crane my arm to grab it, coming up short every time.

My attacker switches up his assault and latches his thick hands around my neck, squeezing and tightening them. "I don't care what you are, you're a fucking sympathizer."

His hold continues to cut off my oxygen supply and my vision blurs even more.

I begin to lose that momentary hope, but when he focuses on choking the life out of me, he rises off my waist, giving me the smallest ability to shift us a little.

Enough for my pleading fingers to dig and scrape and pull the knife within reach.

Consciousness threatens to drag me under with each passing second, but I know I must act, I have to get that fucking knife into my grasp.

The moment I latch onto it, I use every ounce of strength I have left to plunge the sharp end into the man's neck.

His grip loosens on me and his hands frantically move to the knife.

I shove him off me and cough as air fills my lungs.

If I've learned anything from my training with Bo and Wes, it's that sometimes, all it takes is one deadly move to end a fight. Our attacker might still be alive, but it's only a matter of moments before he bleeds out completely.

I scoot myself across the ground to Bo's side and search for any sign of life. His chest rises slowly and then falls, a small but powerful signal that he's still in there. I shake him and like he's just waking from a nap, his eyes open. "About time you wake up."

He sits up and rubs his temple. "What did I miss?" His gaze falls to my face. "You look like shit."

"I thought you were a fucking goner." I will my heart to slow down its pace.

"You can't get rid of me that easily." Bo grunts and rises to his feet, reaching for my hand to bring me to his level, too. He latches onto my shoulder and gives me a firm shake. "Plus, I still have to teach you how to play poker." Bo shakes the shackles latched on his wrists and glances at the fallen men. "I hope one of these fools has a key."

The man I left to bleed out gurgles his last breath and his body goes still.

"Ah man, you had all the fun without me." Bo strolls over and kicks the man onto his back. He rummages through his pockets in search of his freedom.

"Can't say it was much fun." I gently rub at my neck, wincing at the minimal contact on my skin. My entire body aches in some profoundly terrible way. I've had my ass kicked in the past, but this takes it to a new level. It's going to take me days—if not weeks—to recover from these injuries. "What happened to you, anyway? Since when do you fall so easily to two hunters?"

Bo finds what he's looking for and unlocks the cuffs on his wrists. He discards them on top of the man's lifeless body. "Well." He places his hands on his knees and shoves himself upright. "I saw that guy come out of the back of the building, so I started toward you." He motions to the bodies and says, "One of those idiots came out of nowhere. I thought it would be best to deal with him under the cover of the trees. His friend got the best of me and must have whacked me over the head. I don't remember anything after that."

"None of that is like you. It's sloppy."

Bo sighs heavily. "What can I say, I'm not on top of my game."

"You could have gotten yourself killed," I tell him.

Bo remains silent, almost like I struck a nerve somehow. He latches onto one of the men and tosses their body into an overgrown bush. Scanning the vicinity, he searches for another. He grabs the blade out of the guy's throat, wipes the blood onto his pants and once he finds his mark, he throws that man into the concealment of nature. "I'd rather burn their remains, but I don't want to draw any more unwanted attention to us."

As if suddenly remembering what this was all for, I walk over to the supplies I had dropped when I saw Bo in danger. I kneel and retrieve the apples that had scattered and toss the bag back over my shoulder, ignoring the pain that the thing awakens.

"We should get some distance between us and them." Bo comes to my side and grabs the crate, tucking it easily under his arm and securing the other package in the wide grip of his hand.

For the next hour or so, we do exactly that. We zig-zag, crisscross, and walk in silence until the swelling of my face becomes too difficult to see through. I blink and blink, but my lids grow to be small slits I can barely open.

I stop completely and blurt out, "You're going to have to kill me."

"Are you out of your mind?" Bo halts and turns toward me.

I point at myself from head to toe. "I'm worthless in this condition."

"You're worthless in any condition," Bo mouths off.

"No." I shake my head. "Not doing your sarcastic avoidance right now. I'm serious. If you won't do it, I will." I unsheathe the knife from my waistband. Somehow, the idea of killing myself is more unsettling than Bo doing it, but if he won't cooperate, I'll take things into my own hands. "Since when do you have an issue killing someone?"

Bo clenches his jaw and glares at the blade in my hand. "You will not," he growls.

I take a step away from him and grip the thing firmer. "I'm only slowing us down and you know that. I can hardly fucking see. Everything hurts. It'll take me too long to heal. And we cannot afford that kind of delay. We have an advantage, and we need to use it. You don't have a choice in this, Bo."

He matches the distance and then some, appearing right before me. "The hell if I do."

I aim the pointed side at my heart, hoping this is the most effective way to end my life.

Bo places his palm on top of mine and uses his other hand to support my back. "This better fucking work." His voice is strained as he meets my gaze.

Together, with no more argument, we plunge the knife into my chest.

"Thank you," I mutter while maintaining eye contact.

My only hope is that this plan actually works, and I didn't just force my best friend to murder me. Either way, I refuse to be dead weight.

Bo takes my body when I grow weak, and lowers me onto the ground. He holds me in his arms and as my eyes flutter closed, I almost think I see tears well in his. "You better not keep me waiting," he demands.

His words are the last thing I hear before the life leaves my body.

7

WREN

"I don't understand why this isn't working," a man complains.

I keep my eyes shut and my body still in hopes that I can play pretend and listen in on their conversation. I'm tied firmly to a metal chair, it's not like I could go anywhere if I wanted to.

"You're weak, that's why." A woman replies. "I should have known you wouldn't be strong enough to do this."

The more she talks, the more familiar her voice sounds. Through the ringing in my head, I finally realize who it is.

Parla.

My fucking boss. The one who betrayed me and locked me in this torturous place. But if that's her, who is she arguing with?

"I'm sorry, ma'am. It's not without great effort."

Parla grabs onto my chin and tilts my head up at her. "I know you're awake."

I yank free of her grasp and finally take in the room. It's small, but bigger than that of my prior confinement. Similar brick walls and a sturdy door keeping us locked in here. A shiny tray perched atop a stand with various tools. Some are sharp and pointy, and some of the crystal variant. A few vials with no doubt an unfavorable concoction inside. They intend to use both magical and regular physical torture to get what they want out of me.

Good thing they trained me for this kind of thing.

"You want to stop running your mouth and get on with it." I nod toward the selection of devices she can choose between.

Parla folds her arms across her chest and looks down at me through her thick lashes. "It doesn't have to be this way."

"Oh, yeah?" I raise an unamused brow at her.

She's stalling because she knows this type of interrogation won't work on me.

"Tell me what I want to know, and I'll see to it that your sentence is reduced."

"Reduced?" I laugh. "To what? Life in prison? I'll pass."

"It could be worse. I can make it worse. Is that what you want?"

The man she was demeaning fidgets nervously in

the corner of the room, hidden under the shadow cast across his face.

I stare directly at her. "There's nothing you can do to me that hasn't already been done."

Parla unfolds her arms and skims her finger along the edge of the tray. "I'm sure I could get creative."

A grin forms on my already beaten face. "I wish you would."

I didn't rise through the ranks as quickly as I did to claim the title of Furla Ain for nothing. No one handed me anything, I earned it through grit and determination. I became the best of the best. I trained harder than anyone else—put in more time and energy, more blood, sweat, and tears. I gave my soul to the cause because I thought that was the righteous path. Each passing second is a brutal reminder that I was wrong all along. Sure, demons and the like are plaguing our land, but so are the hunters, the purebloods. Both sides are only continuing to fuel the fire of this war.

I'm done being a pawn, a tool used for their advantage. They abused my thirst for vengeance, and I obeyed every order because I was desperate to make a difference. I did, though, that's without a doubt. I've killed countless demons and their bringers, most of them I consumed their essence, making myself that much stronger. Their residual power lingering within me, begging to be let loose. I hold it hostage with no way of setting it free.

"What magician are you working with?" Parla

thoughtfully picks a black stone off the tray and holds it in her palm, examining it.

I sigh, unsure of the angle she's working here. Truthfully, I have no fucking clue what she's talking about. Does she mean the standard-issue witches we use for spelling our safehouses and getting various supplies from? What difference would it make? That person hasn't done anything wrong.

"Rollo," she calls out to the man in the corner.

He appears from the shadows, cowering and keeping his eyes trained on the floor. His old age trails from his snow-white hair to the thickly grooved wrinkles on his brow. His clothes are tattered and worn, his hands filthy. He's not wearing cuffs, but if I had to guess, he isn't here of his own free will.

"Ma'am?" Rollo doesn't look up.

Parla shoves the stone toward him. "You know what to do."

He complies without another word, taking the black rock and coming toward me.

I study him carefully but notice how Parla takes a cautious step back.

Rollo kneels between my restrained legs and lets out a long but quiet breath. He briefly glances up into my eyes and mouths, "I'm sorry."

I clench my jaw and nod stiffly, a silent gesture telling him it's okay, that he can do it.

It's not like either of us has any choice in the matter.

Rollo moves the hair from my right shoulder,

exposing a bit of skin on my chest. He places the cold stone in the open space and mutters a few words. The stone heats up, and with whatever magical spell he spoke, becomes fixed to my body.

A strange sensation floats through me, like little roots taking hold.

This is probably the part where I should fear for my life, but all I feel is a rage that continues to build.

"Was the tether successful?" Parla questions him.

"Yes, ma'am." Rollo stands and moves to her side.

"Give her a taste." Parla grins with each word spoken like she's getting far more enjoyment out of this than she should.

Rollo dips his head even lower, like he's ashamed of being used this way.

That makes two of us.

With a small twist of the wrist, Rollo turns an invisible dial. Immediately, a dull pain consumes my entire body, making it difficult to pinpoint its exact location. You would think the source would stem from the rock adhered to my chest, but no, it's like a million different entry points all buzzing as one.

"More," Parla commands.

Another minor turn increases the voltage flowing through me, but still, I swallow it down and refuse to react. I glare directly at Parla to let her see how unaffected I am.

Does it hurt? Sure. But does she need to know that?

"I said more," she barks at him.

He hesitates despite the approval I had given him to do what she demands.

Parla grows impatient by his lack of enthusiasm and raises her arm, smacking him across the face. "Be of use or I will dispose of you and find someone who is."

I tug at my restraints, eager to bust out of them and choke her until her life leaves her body. "He's doing what you asked, you fucking bitch. It's not his fault I have a high pain tolerance."

Parla's arm twitches like she's considering hitting me, too. "Max capacity," she tells him.

"Ma'am."

She latches onto his shoulder and forces him to face her. "This is your last chance."

"Do it, Rollo. It's fine, really," I reassure him.

He meets my gaze briefly, tears welling in his dark brown eyes before he sinks his head toward the ground, turning his wrist.

The pain slowly increases like he's helping me build a tolerance to it instead of jamming it all into my system at once. Energy fills my veins, and every inch of my body comes alive in the worst way possible. I steady my breath and take it, desperately trying not to give her the reaction she so feverishly desires. My teeth chattering and the sweat building on my brow are the only sign that I'm suffering.

I'm brought back to that day at the warehouse, when I had locked eyes with Wes, our mate bond clicked into place and caused me to make a deadly mistake. I was overcome by demons and left for dead. I had numerous broken bones and wounds that would no doubt result in my death. I couldn't move. All I could do was become one with the agony that was consuming my entire being. I grew familiar with the torment, like it was an old friend I was getting reacquainted with. I accepted my fate.

Part of me was relieved that I would finally see an end to the anguish I carried with me every day since I had run out of that burning house when I was a child. Witnessing death, especially a brutal one, at such a young age changes you, and from that day forward, I was never the same. Nothing has ever been the same.

"Turn it off," Parla tells Rollo. She stalks toward me and grabs my chin, tilting it up to her. "I could listen to your screams all day long, but I have better things to do."

I blink through the sweat that trickled down my face. "I was screaming?"

She huffs. "Don't play dumb with me."

Dizziness threatens to take hold and nausea rises, but I swallow it down and steady my gaze on her. "Anyone ever tell you how boring you are?"

Her grip on my chin tightens. "Who are you working with?"

"I'm Furla Ain, I work for you, dumbass." I yank myself free of her grasp.

"Ms. Oliver." Parla sighs and changes her tactic. "There is a barrier in place, hindering extraction from your person. That block is impossible without magical assistance. So let me ask you again, what witch or warlock has performed this spell on you?"

I allow her accusation to sink in. Extraction? Block? Assistance? I've had no such thing done. How would I even give her the truth if I don't know it myself?

She crosses her arms again and eyes me carefully.

"I have no idea what you're talking about."

"Lies!" she yells, but then quickly composes herself. Parla dusts off invisible debris from her sides and straightens her shirt. "Rollo, max capacity."

He pauses again but with one fierce glare from Parla, he complies, turning the dial on my magical torture device.

My teeth chatter as heat rises within me. A total body electrical field ignites, and pain consumes me. My eyes water and sweat pools between my breasts and in the swell of my back. Hands and legs trembling, I allow it to overtake me, becoming one with the agony. I flip the switch, disassociating from the torment, and give my mind permission to wander, to take me away from this dreadful place. Screams fill the small room, and I drown them out, despite now knowing their source.

I play through the only few memories that bring me joy. Wes, sleeping uncomfortably next to me in his attempt to keep me warm through the night, his possessive and protective nature a characteristic I adore immensely. Dash, making sure I stayed hydrated when I was still considered the enemy, a bright light in this dark and gloomy world; his kindness is something I will cherish until my last breath. Bo, giving me a high-five when we battled together, the stubborn asshole with a subtle compassion he doesn't often let show.

The agony threatens to drag my attention toward it, but I dig in and steer it away. I will not be broken, not by this evil and sadistic bitch.

My chest tightens, bringing me closer to reality than I wish to be. Is this the point of no return? When the line is crossed and I succumb to the attempt to break me? There has to be a threshold, a point where my body can no longer go on—a point where it gives out completely. My will can handle so much, but my actual lifeforce, that's an area I'm unfamiliar with.

The dark stone fixed to my chest pulses, pumping more agonizing pain through me. The end grows near, and I embrace it, giving in to the sweet relief that it will bring. I don't know what will come in the afterlife, but it sure has to be better than this. My only regret is that I have lived my entire life for a hopeless cause. A soldier in an unwinnable war.

"What's happening?" Parla mutters to Rollo.

A scream ripples up and out of my chest, the sound so unfamiliar. My throat aches but it is nothing compared to the pain in the rest of my body.

I grip the arms of the chair and brace myself for what comes next.

Only, instead of death, it's something much more bizarre.

A bright white flash of light fills the room, blinding us all for a split moment. I blink through the illumination and try to find a source of the madness, but it all seems to be radiating from my torso.

I let out another uncontrollable ear-piercing shriek and in the wake of the shock wave, the rock causing my agony splits off from my body and flies across the room, nearly missing Parla and Rollo, and shattering to pieces.

Panting and attempting to slow my racing heart, I lean my head back and soak in the relief of being free of that thing. How it happened? I have no idea. It must have been a malfunction of some sort.

"That's impossible," Rollo whispers.

Parla grills Rollo. "Did you do this? Did you help her?"

"No, I...that's not how this works, ma'am. I cannot do such things."

"If I find out you're lying to me, I will make you suffer worse than this." Parla threatens him and then turns her attention to me. She stands above me, her expression littered with distaste for how this transpired. "You think this is funny, don't you?"

"Hilarious," I struggle to say.

She leans in close, placing both hands on the back of my chair. Steadying her gaze, she smirks. "You're going to find it humorous when I force you to kill your boyfriend and absorb his essence."

My heart stutters, and for the first time since I've

been in this torture chamber, she finally strikes a nerve. "What?"

Parla tilts her head. "Oh, you think I don't know how powerful he is? I might not be able to extract your energy supply yet, but that doesn't mean I can't make you grow in power while I figure out how." She pauses to let that sink in. "In two days, when the moon is at its peak, you will end his life and there will be nothing you can do to stop it from happening."

She stands upright, a smug grin on her stupid face.

A new bout of nausea tumbles around in my stomach. Could what she's saying be true? Is she really going to make me kill Wes and consume his soul? I recall what Franny had said, about no one being killed in a long while, and that of Parla mentioning her having issues extracting power. Does that mean I'm the only one capable of absorbing demonic magic? Is *that* why she's always been so persistent that I do my missions alone, and gives me exceedingly powerful targets? She's been using me as her personal siphon all along and I was none the wiser.

Regardless of the reasoning, one thing is certain— Wes and I are in grave danger and I'm not at all convinced that one, or both, of us are going to make it out of this alive.

8

WES

My beloved is gone, and with her absence, I am helpless and riddled with despair.

I cannot free her of this hell. I have let her down.

My fated mate. The other half of my soul. The person I never thought I'd find, only I found her too late.

If I were honest with her from the start, maybe none of this would have happened. If I never came up with the stupid plan to use her, she would be safe. I could have told her the truth and accepted her rejection, saving us all from this nightmare. Bo could have been reasoned with. Surely he would understand the impossibly rare connection between the two of us. He wouldn't have marked her. She would have healed and left on her own accord, never to be seen again. She would have a future. But no, I was selfish, and now I've doomed her to a worse fate than being mated to a repulsive creature like me.

For that, I will forever be in mourning.

"Someone over there?" A gravelly voice calls through the small, grated opening between our cells.

I lift my head from the shared wall to Wren's empty chamber and look toward the other side but don't respond.

"I can hear you breathing," the man tells me.

I clear my throat. "I'll try to be quieter."

"I haven't had a cellmate in a long time." He pauses and for a moment, I think he's done speaking completely. "You must be powerful if they put you in there."

I let out a small chuckle. "That's doubtful." Glancing at the shackles on my wrist, I'm reminded once again of how powerless I am. Even my beast side has forsaken me.

"Just because they've suppressed your abilities doesn't mean they're any less there. No, they're simply lying dormant, ready to rise to the surface."

"Seems unlikely, but I appreciate the words of encouragement."

The man moves around in his room, perhaps finding a more comfortable way to engage with me. "May I ask?"

"I'd rather you didn't." There are very few who know the truth about what I am, and even then, I can't be certain I know much about myself at all. I was orphaned at an early age, my birth parents a mystery I've never solved. I was taken in by a kind woman who raised me and despite not sharing blood, she was my mother.

In the perpetual state of war our realm is in, there has been no opportunity to research, and even if there was, most demonic historical centers have been burned to the ground. Our history has gone up in flames, diminished to the burning embers and waning ash.

"I came to Prania to seek refuge," he confesses.

"Did you find what you were looking for?" There's no hiding the sarcasm in my inquiry.

He laughs bluntly. "In a way, yes. But what's that old saying, 'you trade in one set of problems for another'?"

"I can't imagine a reality where I would choose being here over anywhere else." Prania is home, but it is also a lost cause.

"After being here a few years, I can agree with you there."

I crane my neck toward the voice coming through the other side of my room. Did I hear him correctly? *A few years?* That can't be true. Prania has been closed off to any other realm for far longer than that. It's inescapable. No one comes in or out. The hunters made damn sure of that when they shut it off and started eradicating anyone but themselves.

I push myself up off the floor and weakly walk over to him. With a thud, I slide down the wall and resume my pitiful existence near this strange man. "How is that possible?"

"Which part?"

"How did you get here?"

He lets out a long breath. "Like I said, I was running from something. I called in a favor, hoping to travel to any realm other than my own. Little did I know that I'd end up here."

"A favor? With whom?"

"Someone more powerful than me. Although, I do wonder if I would have fared better had I stayed put."

I shouldn't entertain this conversation, but if what he's saying is true, that means it could actually be possible to escape this realm. That is, if we can find a way out of this prison. Something I've been searching for my entire life, right here just out of reach.

The man continues, "I've done a lot of thinking while locked in here. Reflecting on the things I've done in the past. Solitude will do that to a person."

"And what have you learned?"

He exhales again. "For one, it's okay to be wrong. To make bad decisions and regret them. To realize that maybe you were the villain after all." He repositions himself again. "I hurt a lot of people. I lied; I stole. I let even more down, and it was all for nothing. I thought I was taking back what was mine, but I was just being a bully. A selfish and inconsiderate power-hungry jackass."

Each of his words are layered with guilt and

remorse, and if I had to guess, he means every one of them.

"I went through withdrawals when I came to this realm. It was painful. But it was a necessary purge I didn't know I desperately needed. I had gone so long with stolen power, that I felt uncomfortable with just my own. I was dependent on it, and I grew too familiar with what wasn't mine that I couldn't recognize the person I was without it. The longer I went without, the harder it became. And then all of a sudden, there was one day when it wasn't as difficult. With each passing day, I grew more okay with myself. That's when I realized the horrors of what I had done and what it cost me, and so many others.

"I want to make amends. To right my wrongs, but the time for that has passed."

A glimmer of hope sparks in my chest. "What makes you so sure?" First, it was the guard showing me a small kindness, and now my cellmate has information on how to get out of Prania. Either the fates are truly out to screw me over, or there might be some chance of surviving this.

"You alluded to it yourself about being powerless in here."

"Not if we work together." It's an unlikely alliance, but if it means getting out of here, I'd align with the devil himself. "You're a witch?"

"In my past life, yes."

I shake my head. "That isn't something you ever shake, sir."

"No need for the formalities, son. You can call me Tremont."

"Tremont," I repeat. "I'd shake your hand, but our accommodations don't exactly allow for it. I'm Wes."

"They are rather...confining, aren't they?" He laughs gently. "You call out a name in your sleep sometimes. Is that who's in the next cell?"

My chest tightens and if my hound were present, his possessiveness would rise to the surface. It's strange not having him constantly causing a commotion in my head, but my reflexes somehow know how he would react in most situations. "Yes," is all I respond.

He takes a long moment before saying anything else. "Wes?"

"Hm?" My eyes grow heavy as the exhaustion threatens to take hold. My wounds are healing much slower than normal, and the cuffs on my wrists prevent any of my powers from rising to the surface. Between the intermittent torturing and the lack of proper hydration and food, my body is fighting to perform at even a minimal capacity.

"This wing, the one we're in right now. It houses the prison's most profound creatures. They wouldn't have put you or her here if they didn't fear you. They're trying to break you. To get in your head. You mustn't allow that to happen."

That's easier said than done. I'm supposed to be

this wrecking force and here I am, weak and struggling to stay alive. They've nearly made me mortal, and yet are treating me like a beast.

Why don't they just kill me and get it over with?

A loud creaking sounds from the cell next to me, snapping me out of my stupor and sending me scuttling across the floor to the other side.

"Wren," I plead with the once empty space.

A thud is followed by the door closing, and then the faint sniffling of my angel.

"Wren," I say again. "Are you okay?"

Shuffling ensues and then a dainty hand weaves its way through the grated area. "I'm okay."

Her skin is cold and clammy to the touch, and when I latch onto her completely, I notice she's trembling.

The door to Tremont's cell opens and by the sound of it, he's next in line for an afternoon of torment.

"What did they do to you?" I press myself on my side and desperately try to peer into her cell at her.

"Nothing I can't handle," she tells me with her eyes pinched closed and sweat coating her forehead.

Wren's black hair sticks to her cheeks and I wish for nothing more than to brush it away, to pull her to my chest and keep her safe from any harm that may come to her. To be the man she needs, that she deserves.

"I'm so sorry," I whisper while grazing my lips against her knuckles. I kiss every inch of her I can reach, apologizing with each one of them.

"Hey." She peers through her heavy lids. "We're in this together, okay?"

"Yeah." I should have anticipated this. I should have protected her. I should have done *something* to stop this from happening.

"Speaking of…" Wren opens her eyes wider. "I need in there."

An automatic grin forms on my face. "You and me both."

"No, I'm serious." She brings her other hand to her mouth to cover a nasty cough.

My breath hitches. "Is that blood?"

Wren blinks a few times and examines her hand. "That's nothing." She wipes it on her side and ignores my growing concern. "I have an idea, but we have to be in the same room."

"What is it? The idea?" Not that I'd say no to not having a wall separating us.

"I'd rather just try it, but we have to find a way. The guard, the one that we discussed, maybe we could convince him to give us a few minutes."

"I don't want to put you in any more danger."

She narrows her gaze at me. "I think the time for that has passed, don't you think? Desperate times call for desperate measures. And if I have to put a little faith in one of them, it's a risk I'm willing to take. Especially if it means the possibility of gaining any kind of advantage." She draws in a breath. "Besides, stop pretending like I can't defend myself. I understand that you feel that need, but I've been doing fine without you this long."

"And look where that got you." Before I allow the guilt to continue to sink in, I shift the topic of conversation. "I met my other cellmate."

"Yeah?"

I nod and lower my voice. "He's a witch. But get this...he's only been in Prania a few years."

"That's impossible."

"That's what I thought."

"You believe him?"

"He had a rather compelling story, and I can't for the life of me come up with a reason why he would lie about it."

"Wes, if that's true..."

"I know."

Her eyes dart back and forth like she's considering a million different possibilities. Finally, she stops and focuses on me. "Do you think they're okay?"

Dash and Bo.

The two of them have been in my thoughts almost as much as Wren. They're my family and there is no telling how dangerous things have been for them trapped inside enemy territory.

"Do you still feel him?" I flit my attention to the faded but still present mark on her neck.

Wren brings her fingers to it, skimming along the ridges. "I do," she whispers.

"If they've survived the initial fallout, I'm sure

they'll be fine." My mind wanders to the close calls we've experienced together, none of them quite like this, but they never failed to survive then, so I have to hope they will do the same now. "And D...at least we can worry a little less about him now."

"That doesn't mean they aren't suffering." Her body tenses with each word. "Just because he *can* come back..."

"I know," I tell her. The idea of Dash dying over and over to stay alive isn't something any of us want to imagine. Luckily, he and Bo have each other, the same way Wren and I do.

We'll get through this—together.

Wren wiggles her hand back over to her side and pushes herself onto her butt. "We can't afford to waste any more time."

I grip at the grate between us. "You need to rest." Oh, what I would give to whisper a few words and give her reprieve from her injuries. Sure, it takes a strain on me, but I'd gladly endure it if it meant she was better. The fated mate bond we share allows me to control her, and with that, I can mend her wounds if I align my request correctly. By setting my intentions properly, I can absorb her pain with just a touch. I've abused these powers in the past, hindering her healing progress and even disallowing her from being able to speak. That one was a mistake on my behalf, which could have resulted in her death. I hate myself for continuing to put her in harm's way.

That's why I leapt out of those woods that day. I had been suppressing Wren's powers because I worried if she gained her full strength that she would leave us. I could have let her be taken and then work with the guys to figure out a way to save her, but I couldn't send her in here without her strength. She never would have made it through the first round of interrogation with my compulsion still intact. It put me in danger, and exposed the lie that she had told, but there was no way my beast would allow her to face this on her own. If she was going down, so were we.

Only, he isn't here to help us—and that alone is not something I anticipated.

"I'll rest when I'm dead." Wren rises to her feet and walks over to the other side of her cell.

I strain to see through the small barrier. She whispers something but I can't make it out. My enhanced hearing is also suffering now that I'm locked in here.

My heart picks up its pace, thudding wildly in my chest. I wish to be over there, right beside her, ready to throw myself in front of her if any danger comes her way. Even without my hound present, I'm still territorial and protective over her. That natural reaction coincides with being completely captivated by a person. I would do anything for her; give my life for her.

A couple minutes pass of hushed conversation, and Wren tears herself away from the wall but doesn't return to me. Instead, she goes toward her door, and taps on it gently. Once. Twice. Then three rapid but quiet knocks.

I stand, my hand pressed against the stone between us, my breath caught in anticipation of the unknown. What if she summons the wrong person? What if her plan blows up in her face and makes our situation somehow worse? If that's at all possible. My soul can't continue to bear the weight of seeing her abused and tortured when it knows with certainty that all of this is my fault.

Her lock turns slowly, grinding with each minimal rotation. The door groans open, and with it, I'm left wondering which outcome we're about to experience.

9

BO

I really love killing people.

I mean, I'm not kidding. There's something exciting about ending the life of someone who deserves it. Watching the light leave their eyes and knowing you were the one to snuff out their flame.

I've done it more times than I could count—not that the number would matter anyway.

But even knowing Dash will resurrect, the weight of his demise comes at no less of a gut punch. I shoved a knife into his heart and held him as he slumped to the ground and his body finally gave in to the injury.

And now, I watch over him with bated breath as I wait for him to come back.

I didn't want to assist him, but if he did it himself, he might have missed and caused himself more pain than necessary. He gave me no choice in the matter, and despite him having a compelling case for wanting to die, it still didn't make it any easier to go through with.

I've never been one to need or desire the company of others. I've grown fond of my time alone. I've sort of resented Wes for his insistence that we stick together, and that only grew when Dash came along. I've been bitter and callous toward them. I thought they were holding me back and contributing to the stresses of my existence.

I didn't realize how very wrong I was until Wes and Wren were taken, and Dash decided to end his own life, leaving me here without any of them to annoy me. Maybe, just maybe, I don't hate them as much as I thought I did.

Because why else would I be genuinely concerned that Dash might not resurrect?

If he doesn't, I might as well off myself, too. On the chance that Wes and Wren break out of Rock Bridge, they'll murder me for what I permitted Dash to do. And I'm not entirely sure I would blame them. Dash is the one innocent in our little group of castaways, and we must protect him at all costs.

I keep an eye on our surroundings, noting every leaf that falls or gust of wind that floats by, stirring the branches of the trees. If one weren't running for their life, this dense forest might actually be considered peaceful. But like Wren's disarming beauty, what's under the surface is far more deadly.

I press my hand to my chest and close my eyes,

conjuring the connection I have to her. It's difficult to access, but with great effort, I can faintly sense her—meaning she's still alive. Wes, I'm not so sure. But one of them is better than none, and just because I can only confirm her life, doesn't mean Wes is any less alive. It's hard to imagine a fierce beast like him being taken down without one hell of a fight—and with the two of them together, Rock Bridge doesn't know what it's messing with. Although, the sooner we can break into the place and free them, the better. There's no telling what kind of torment they're experiencing.

A guttural growl rumbles in my chest at imagining someone hurting Wren. I once wanted to end her life, and now, the thought of it drives me nearly mad.

I recall the warmth of her body as she pressed it against me when she was trying to make Wes angry. It was all an act, but still, it stirred things I've been fighting to suppress. It's one thing to *tolerate* a hunter, but it's another to...

My thoughts are halted by a crackling, and then a flicker of flame.

Relief washes over me as Dash's transformation begins. How would I have explained to Wes and Wren that I accidentally on purpose killed their sweet ginger?

It takes another moment before Dash's body completely catches fire. It burns bright and hot for another long minute, and then a solid encasement covers him. The dark smoke flutters up and through the trees, a signal that we should get out of here sooner rather than later. The hunters tracking us will surely pick up on any sign of life not sanctioned by their own authority. Especially when they realize there are dead bodies of their comrades stuffed in the bushes outside their encampment.

The shell cracks slowly, like Dash is taking his good ol' time.

I sigh and cross my arms. "Today," I tell him.

Watching him resurrect the first time was incredible, a gift from the universe when we needed it most, but now I'd rather him hurry up.

Finally, his hand bursts through the center and shoves away the debris. Dash rises to the seated position and dusts the excess off his shoulders.

"About time." I reach over and ruffle his head, knocking off a bit of the molt.

"It worked." He grins at me and holds his arms out to examine his injury-free body. "I feel great." Dash touches his face, and then his chest, where I had shoved a knife through it not too long ago.

I extend the thing to him, handle first. "Here."

"Right. Thanks." Dash stands, brushing himself off more before taking the knife from me and tucking it away on his person. Glancing down at the remaining embers of his transformation, he says, "Let's get out of here." He steps out of the debris and tosses the back-pack over his shoulder. "I'm starving."

"Me too, bud, me too."

"You didn't eat?" He pauses and narrows his gaze at me.

"And miss the show?" I tuck the crate under my arm and grip the other parcel in my hand. Without lingering any longer, I take off away from our campsite.

"Aw, you were worried about me." Dash jogs to catch up.

"Was not." I huff.

"Admit it, you don't hate me as much as you let on."

I glare at him out of the corner of my eye. "I never said I hated you."

Dash breaks out into a shit-eating grin. "I knew it."

"We need to get out of here."

"Sure, change the subject." He nudges me with his elbow.

"Until we learn more about whatever your abilities are..." I look at him briefly. "We should probably hold off on resorting to death."

"What, you think it has a limit?"

I shrug and continue stalking further from the remains that could get us caught. "Nature always has a give and take. My powers don't come without restraint, some exchange to maintain the balance. Wes is no different. There's always a *price*."

"Oh." Dash looks to the ground, watching his feet with each step. A silence falls between us until his curiosity overtakes him. "Like what kind of price?"

My stomach grumbles, reminding me of one of the costs. "Energy."

"Energy?" he echoes.

"We all need substance to survive. Whether it be food, blood, or flesh. Each creature is different, but when you use your powers, you lose those reserves quicker, and they must be replenished. Sometimes, it's not so easily restored."

"What do you mean?"

I grip onto a small tree on the side of a ridge and lift myself over the edge, careful not to drop the packages that Dash risked his life for.

He grunts and struggles, but manages to maneuver himself up and over, too.

I close my eyes and breathe deeply, sensing our surroundings. The cool air floats through my chest and reassures me that we are far enough away to take a quick break.

"Are you okay?" Dash whispers at my side.

I peek through one lid at him. "We should eat."

Finding a few discarded logs to set our supplies on, we dig into the stolen goods. I rip the top off the crate and nearly salivate at the sight of meat. I yank out two equally sized dried hunks and extend one toward Dash. When he doesn't take it immediately, I turn to him, watching as he unzips his pack and fumbles with the contents.

My mouth literally drops open upon seeing the loaf of bread he pulls out.

With a giant grin on his face, he shoves it in my direction while taking his piece of protein.

I bring the thing to my nose, breathing in the fresh scent. Only one thing in this world smells better than bread...

My chest tightens at the idea of her being starved and tortured, and here I am, drooling over some carbs. Still, if I stand any chance of saving Wren and Wes, I have to fuel my reserves.

"Did I do good?" Dash chews his meat and leans against a tree.

I rip a small corner off the loaf and hand the rest to Dash. "I could pretty much kiss you over this." I lift the piece that I kept for myself. "But we should ration. There's no telling how long we'll be out here, and when we'll come across food again."

Dash nods, shoving the thing back into his bag and pulling out a bright red apple. "I got a few of these, too."

Setting my provisions to the side, I take the apple from him, gripping both sides and snapping the thing in two. I give him one half and keep the other, placing it with the glorious meal we've put together. If only we had some cheese to go with it.

Cheese.

Immediately, my mind assaults me with the memory of her, nibbling on a hunk of the salty substance, basically smiling and buzzing the same way I do with bread.

Dash interrupts my thoughts. "Can I ask you a question?"

"You just did."

Dash rolls his eyes. "You know what I mean."

"I'm waiting." I force myself to chew slowly and savor each bite of the bread.

"Why didn't you...*eat* those hunters? You know, like drain them of their blood the way you normally do."

I inhale deeply, considering my response. "We were in a hurry."

"We're always in a hurry, and that's never stopped you before."

Gritting my teeth, I glare at the questioning redhead. "It was different this time."

"Bo?"

"Yes, Dash?"

"Have you at all? Since..."

He doesn't have to say another word for me to comprehend his train of thought. Since I marked Wren; since I tasted her sweet essence; since I sank my teeth into her flesh, and everything changed. "No."

It's the first time I've truly acknowledged it, to myself, to anyone else. I've known all along that the course of my existence had altered that day, but I've done everything I could to evade whatever was set in motion. I kept to the ruse of hating her, of wanting to end her life, because that's how it should have been. Instead, I gravitated toward her, curious about the connection I felt for her. My hatred for her turned into pure rage for anyone who so much as glanced in her direction.

"Do you want to talk about it?" Dash pries a bit further.

"No." I shut him down. It's not like I'd know what to say anyway. I can't seem to make sense of any of this myself. I shouldn't feel the way I do for her, and yet, I find it all-consuming.

"We're going to get her back, Bo. I don't know how, but we will."

I sink my teeth into the flesh of the apple and ignore the unfamiliar concern that settles in my core. It's unlike anything I've ever known to worry about another. Even as close as Wes and Dash have been to me, I've never felt quite like *this*. No, this is foreign, new, and a bit terrifying.

Eyeing that other package Dash had retrieved, I snatch it and tear open the side, desperate for something to distract me from my *feelings*. Blinking a few times, I allow my mind to catch up. Carefully, I pull one of the many small things out, tilting it around in my hand to take a better look.

"What is that?" Dash steps closer.

"Our saving grace." Or our demise, but I don't tell him that part.

One thing is certain though, I will do whatever it takes to make sure Dash's words ring true. We will save her if it's the last thing I do—even if that means I die in the process.

10
WREN

I knock on the door just like Franny told me to, holding my breath in anticipation of the unknown. If I choose to do nothing, I'm a dead woman, so what's the harm in being bold and taking risks?

Wes's beast side came to me, told me that I have to act in order to save us both. He alluded that we must consummate our mate bond for Wes's powers to return. And without those, we stand no chance of making it out of here alive. We need every advantage we can get, even if that means trusting a stranger. In this case, trusting two. Franny seems genuine, but there's no telling if it's an act to let our guards down. I don't really know much about this guard, but Wes is slightly convinced he could potentially be an ally. Given his connection to Franny, I hope it's true.

The lock on my door creaks, and the latch is turned slowly.

I step out of its way and ready myself for a battle if need be. One way or another, I am going to get to Wes.

A man, perhaps a bit younger than me, looks through the opening. "Yes?"

I study the softness of his expression, the hint of concern lingering on his brow. His demeanor is nothing like the other guards—completely absent of that volatile hatred and thirst for inflicting pain. He shifts his gaze toward the hallway and then back at me.

If I were in better shape, I could easily overpower him. But I'm not, and that would only cause more chaos.

"I..." My voice cracks and I clear my throat. "I need a favor, please."

The man doesn't get angry, he doesn't shove in and beat me with his baton, he doesn't even seem irritated at my request.

"My authority is limited in here, miss."

"I just need five minutes, that's all I ask."

He raises his brow. "Of what, exactly?"

I force myself not to glance down at the knife at his waist. The urge to fight is strong, but I must be smarter, more strategic, if I want to get out of this mess. I tilt my head toward Wes's cell. "I need to see him."

He shakes his head but keeps his voice low. "No, not happening."

Tears well in my eyes, partially from the possibility

of this plan failing, and from wanting to appeal to his empathetic side. "I don't think he has much longer. He's not healing from his injuries."

"It's too dangerous, if someone catches you in there, it's not only your head, it's mine, too." He tugs on the handle. "The risk is too high."

I shove my foot in the open space so he can't shut the door. "I just want to say goodbye, face to face. Please, I'm begging you."

I take his pause to run a few scenarios through my head. I could use what little strength I have to kick him in the chest, knocking him to the ground. If I don't render him unconscious, I'd have to kill him, because I couldn't gamble with him stopping me. I'd have to figure out which key unlocks Wes's door, and hope I could get in without drawing the attention of any other guards. And then there's the possibility that the mate bond doesn't ignite Wes's powers. But if it doesn't, at least we'll be together when we meet our demise, and that alone is enough to make all this worth it.

The man tilts his watch toward him. He clenches his jaw and lets out a breath. "You have two minutes, that's it, okay?"

Hope bursts throughout me. "Yes." I bob my head up and down. "Yes. Thank you."

He stiff-arms the door and stares directly into my eyes. "You follow my orders and do not run, deal?"

In another life, I would have lied, told him what he wanted to hear, and then turned on him the second the opportunity presented itself, but I can't afford to be that way, not when the variables are constantly changing. So instead, I tell him the truth, because that's all I can afford right now. "Deal."

I slither through the small opening and into the damp, empty hallway. My thoughts are taken back to the dream I had, only this time, the guard is guiding me along, not the hound. Together, we pause in front of Wes's chamber, my heart beating wildly in my chest for a million different reasons. My head goes fuzzy at the overwhelming nature of the endless outcomes that could come to fruition.

What if I'm wrong? What if this causes more harm than good? What if I've used up my one courtesy with this random guard? What if he gets caught and is taken to another post, leaving us with the rabid other men who would rather beat us than show us the slightest kindness? What if I ruin whatever Franny and this guard have because I was selfish in needing this time with Wes?

But, what if it's the difference between us surviving or not?

"Two minutes, the clock is ticking." The guard slides the key into Wes's lock and opens the door, moving me through the small space and closing it behind me.

I blink through the darkness to adjust my eyes and gasp when a large form completely consumes my body.

I relax into him and wrap my arms tighter around his strong form. "Wes," I breathe.

He pulls away, gripping my face in his hands. His eyes dart back and forth to mine. "Are you fucking crazy?"

"We don't have long." I stand on my tiptoes and brush my lips against his.

Wes stiffens and hesitates, but gives in to my kiss, deepening it with a gentle intensity.

I tug him tighter, and he winces under my minimal force, reminding me exactly why I'm here. "Hey." I break from his mouth and stare at him. I trail my hands down to his waist and unbutton his pants.

"What are you doing?" His chest heaves from the labor he's already exerted.

"Do you trust me?" I ask him.

"With every fiber in my being."

I reach up and skim my hand over his battered face. "Then drop your pants and sit down against the wall."

Wes locks his eyes with mine and contemplates the severity of my request. For a split second, I'm convinced he's going to say no, to protest and persuade me to come to my senses. But despite my weakened condition and my frantic state, there's nothing more that I want than to be close to him. In our final moments, I consider that a gift from the universe—and a twisted cruelty by the fates.

Going to work on my own bottoms, I drag them

over my ass, peeling them off my swollen and dirty body.

Wes watches me intensely as I stroll over to him, straddling his legs and kneeling over his lap. Just the minimal skin-to-skin contact is enough to send fireworks dancing across my flesh.

He shakes his head faintly. "You don't know what you're doing, Wren."

My name on his lips is another burst of pleasure in this torture chamber.

I graze my thumb over his bottom lip, tugging it down. "Yes, I do."

His erection pulses beneath me but he doesn't move otherwise. Wes remains still, allowing me to be the one in control.

If we were anywhere but here, I would take my time exploring his body, building us both up to magical bliss. I'd savor this experience with him.

His lips part and he sighs. "I wanted this to be somewhere romantic..."

"What's more romantic than life or death?" I force a smile, although I'm sure it comes out more pathetic than I intend. "Do you want this?" I ask him.

It's then that he finally raises his arm, hovering his hand beside my cheek, the width of his palm encasing the side of my face. "Only if you do."

I position myself closer, one arm wrapping around his neck, the other going between my legs to grip his shaft. I suppress my surprise by locking my mouth onto his. Our tongues dart out to dance with each other like long-lost lovers, moving in a way that would make you think we'd done this a million times before.

The room melts away and it's only me and Wes left behind.

No danger. No worries. No enemies.

Only, I'm not that fucking foolish.

I slide further, running the length of him over my slit. Without breaking from his kiss, I kneel taller and situate his cock at my entrance.

"Wren?" Wes breathes into my mouth. "There's no going back from this."

I pull his lip between my teeth. "I don't want to."

"The mate bond, I won't be able to resist it." His voice cracks with concern.

I tilt his neck up so he can meet my gaze. "That's the point." Not wasting another second, I push myself down, forcing his thickness inside of me. I fight the urge to drop my head back in both pain and pleasure and maintain my eye contact with him.

His lids flutter and his breath catches. "My love." And like he finally gives in to the temptation, he glides his hands over my thighs and grips onto my waist, digging his fingers into my skin and guiding me up and down.

My heart nearly leaps out of my chest when I catch a faint flicker of red spark in his eyes, but he shifts his focus before I confirm or deny.

"Keep looking at me," I urge him.

A light knock sounds on the door—a warning that our time is almost up.

"Wes, I need you to come for me."

"What?"

I tighten myself around his cock and increase the tempo, desperate to make sure this plan has any chance of succeeding. I don't know the intricacies of a mate bond, but I'd do anything to lock it in place.

"I want you to..."

But I cut him off before he can finish his statement. "This isn't about me right now, it's about you. It's about us. And what I want more than anything..." I press my mouth along his and try to persuade him with my kiss. "Is for you to come."

"Wren," he breathes.

I wrap my hand around the base of his neck, applying soft but firm pressure. "Do you want to please me?"

He nods while dragging one of his hands from my waist and placing it on top of mine, intensifying the force of my grasp. "Yes."

"Then make me yours, Wes, I'm begging you."

In a flash, I'm on my back and Wes is still between my legs. He keeps a hand under my head to protect it from the cold, hard floor, while the other is planted firmly to the side to keep the brunt of his weight off me. He could easily crush me if he wanted to—our bodies are drastically different in size in almost every way, and yet somehow, we fit perfectly together.

Wes closes his eyes and thrusts inside of me, his girth stretching me open.

My own body surprises me with what it's capable of taking.

"Wes." I dig my nails into his back and drag him closer and closer.

An explosion sounds in the distance, rattling the walls of our chamber, but it's no match to the eruption I feel building in my core.

Wes blinks up at me, flickers of red sparking his irises.

My mouth drops open and I gasp. "There you are," I whisper.

"Am I hurting you?" Wes pauses momentarily and the crimson begins to fade.

A tear betrays me by rolling down my cheek. "No." Because no amount of pain would ever *not* be worth this moment. "Keep going."

"Are you sure?"

"Wes, I swear to the fates, if you don't..."

Wes grins and crashes his lips onto mine, kissing me with an intensity unlike anything I've ever felt. His cock hardens and a moment later, he moans into my mouth, his orgasm finally crashing over him and into me. He slows his pace while he drags it out and stares into my eyes.

The glowing red orbs I thought I'd never see again glare back at me, sending me spiraling into my own climax. I pulsate around his shaft and my entire body trembles with the aftershock. Together, we ride out this temporary bliss until we're two euphoric bodies left here in this dirty cell.

Only now, Wes's beast side has joined us.

Wes presses a soft kiss on my lips and sits up, gently pulling himself out of me. "Fuck, Wren, you're bleeding."

I sit up on my elbows and revel in the surrealness of the fading moment. "What did you expect? You're built like a…"

He raises a brow. "Like a…?"

I shake my head and chuckle. "You'll have to ask me again when I'm not high on you."

Wes places his hand just along the outside of where he just wrecked. He mutters a few words and within seconds the pain subsides, and I'm left with nothing but pleasure.

"You did it." I fully sit upright. "You fucking did it."

But as I move closer, Wes stumbles a bit. "That took more out of me than it normally does."

"Wait." I catch up to the meaning behind his words. "It takes a toll on you when you heal me?"

Wes nods. "Usually it's manageable."

I climb to his side and hold his face in my hands. "No more, okay? Not until we're out of here, and we're far, far away. You use every bit of strength you have to tend to your own wounds."

His jaw clenches under my touch. "I can't do that."

I graze my thumb along his skin. "Yes, you can. Promise me, Wes."

His fiery gaze meets mine.

"Promise me," I repeat with more conviction.

"Please don't make me." Pain lingers in his voice.

"You have to," I insist. "You're our only chance of making it out of here. I need you to be strong for both of us."

Something I've never done before, give someone else the power to control whether I live or die. I've gone my entire life fighting my own battles, waging my own wars—but right now, I've conceded to this hauntingly beautiful man in front of me.

"Okay."

I grip his pants and toss them onto his lap and crane my neck to find where I had discarded my own. "That was more than two minutes, the guard must have gotten distracted by whatever that explosion was." I stand and slip into my leather bottoms, securing them in place. "But he gave us enough time to get the mate bond in place."

Wes doesn't respond as he finishes getting dressed.

"What aren't you telling me?" I ask him.

He leans against the wall, crossing his arms over his chest. He's trying to shut me out, but now that his powers are somewhat in place, I'd wager he can no longer lie to me. That's why he didn't want me to make him promise, because his word to me is something he cannot break.

The door to Wes's cell cracks open. "Time's up, you need to go."

Wes kicks off the hard surface and rushes over to me, his hands find my shoulders and guide me toward the opening. He leans down to kiss me, but I evade his lips.

"Wes?" My heart pounds wildly at the unknowns filling my mind.

"You can't get caught, Wren." He continues to move my stiff body.

"The mate bond..." It's the only thing I can think of that would make sense. Sex wasn't the only variable in consummating the link between us.

The guard latches onto my arm and tugs me through the opening. "We have to hurry."

"I'm sorry," Wes murmurs as the door closes us off from each other.

Anger and sadness and confusion consume me.

Was all of that for nothing? If I failed the mission, maybe we really are doomed after all.

Parla told me that I would have to kill Wes and consume his essence and I thought the only way to stop that from happening was to follow through with the dream I had of Wes's beast. To grant him the power to free us of this nightmare. Wouldn't his beast have told me if there was another step in the plan? Or what if I was woken up prior to getting to that part and I've been a fool this entire time thinking it would be *that* easy?

It's clear that *some* of his powers are back, but with

how sporadic they came and went in those few moments, there's no telling how long they will stick around. My only hope is that it's long enough for Wes to heal, to become strong enough to at least save himself.

But the sinking pit in my stomach alerts me that hope is a useless thing.

II
WREN

"What was that commotion?" I ask the guard before we reach my cell.

"Not sure yet. But you're lucky, it bought you a few extra minutes." He slides the key into my door and tugs me toward the opening. "Sector twelve is on high alert. Guard activity will no doubt be increased as soon as they clean that mess up. I'll do my best to stay positioned over here, but I cannot control where they send me." He flits his gaze toward the empty hallway and then back at me. "Get in."

Lucky. More like cursed.

"Why are you doing this? Being kind to me, to him?" I nod my head toward Franny's chamber. "To her?"

"Because good and evil are not what they want us to believe. Now hurry, before we both get caught." He nudges me through the threshold and shuts the door behind me. "I hope you got what you were after, because that can't happen again."

My heart rips in two at the weight of his words and the realness of the situation. I was convinced I would succeed, that my crazy and spur-of-the-moment plan would work. But with each passing second, the pit in my gut grows, reminding me that nothing in my life has ever been easy, so why would I expect it to start now? Doubt continues to creep in, and no matter how hard I try to fight it, it becomes all-consuming. I've always figured out how to get out of tight situations, but what if this is the one time my brain and brawn fail me for good? And for the first time in my life, it's not just my own ass on the line. It's Wes's. It's Bo's and Dash's. It's Franny's. People I never thought I'd have—taken too soon.

"Did it work?" A small voice calls out to me from the meager opening between our cells.

I exhale and make my way over to her, leaning against the wall and sliding down onto my ass. "I don't think so." I close my eyes and let the weight of my head fall back, bringing my knees forward and holding myself tightly.

"Wren...?"

"Yeah, kid?"

"I have a bad feeling."

"You and me both." My lids open in a flash. "Wait.

Like a *feeling* feeling?" I lower my tone to a whisper. "A banshee one?"

"There's a burning under the surface of my skin. An itch in the back of my throat. A pulsing throb in my skull. An overwhelming sense of doom. I cannot shake it, and it only continues to grow in intensity." She pauses. "I don't know how I know this...but it's big."

"Big like a powerful demon big?"

"Maybe. I can't be sure."

"Wes," I breathe.

"What did you say?"

"Nothing." I shake my head. "Do your powers give you any insight on *when* it might happen?"

"No, not really. It's all muddled and being in here doesn't help matters. I'd venture to assume we don't have long."

Bringing my hands to my head, I rub my temples. It can't end like this; I won't allow it. I haven't fought and trained my entire life to die at the hands of the monsters who created me. I refuse to let Wes or Franny succumb to them either. I have to do fucking *something*.

Shuffling from across the room steals my attention. *Wes.* The fierce beast who holds more power than any other creature in this prison. "Wren," he calls out to me.

"Franny, I'm going to figure this out. I won't let you die in here." And because I need her to understand how serious I am, I add, "I promise."

"Don't make promises you can't keep, and regardless, you don't owe me anything."

At the end of the day, no one really owes anyone anything, but I have a lifetime of mistakes to make up for, and if I can begin by helping her, I'll do it without question. A month ago I would have been selfish and only focused on saving myself. Now, I'm sickened with the reality of that being no way to live.

"Will you keep me posted if anything changes?" I ask her.

"Of course."

I crawl from one side of my cell to the other to join Wes. Is it possible for a heart to break just from the thudding concern of not knowing how to fix the unfixable?

"I'm sorry," he blurts out as soon as I approach.

"How do we finalize it, Wes? You have to tell me, please." Because his beast side very well could be the only thing that has the potential of saving us all. Without it, we're a lost cause.

He remains quiet despite being the one that called me over here.

"Wes." I calm the rage that builds within me and focus on the severity of my next statement. "We don't have long. Something bad is going to happen, and I don't think I'm strong enough to fight."

"Let me heal you." His voice cracks with each word.

"No." It's not even an option in my mind. If Wes gives me some of his power, then he loses it for himself.

Our best bet is to bank on Wes mending from his own injuries and conjuring his beast side. We need every ounce we can get and cannot afford for him to heal my measly injuries.

"Wren…"

"Damn it, Wes, you're not going to convince me otherwise." I fight the rage that builds within. "Do you not understand how careless you're being? Stop for a second and think logically. If you want to help me, you have to help yourself. That's the only way. So have a little chat with your beast side and tell him to step up his fucking game."

Another explosion sounds in the distance, this time a bit closer than earlier.

"If we're going to make it out of this, I need you to do everything you can to unleash your beast side." Never in my wildest dreams would I imagine that I'd be convincing a demon to embrace his demonic nature and truly desire it to happen.

Once upon a time, I hated all things demon. Am I still furious that they stole my family from me? Absolutely, but being lied to and conditioned to hate a species because of it pisses me off even more. They leveraged my hatred to fuel their agenda, whatever it may be. I've been used as a puppet, a soldier who was disposed of the second I deviated from their orders. I gave them my life. I fought and killed and did their bidding, and for what? Where has it gotten me? Nowhere but locked in prison with trust issues and a deep-seated thirst for getting revenge on who actually deserves it.

The demons of Prania are not the real monsters—the fucking administration running this place are. A bunch of hypocritical, power-hungry cunts.

That familiar sound of my door unlocking draws my attention toward it. Given it hasn't been long since I arrived, I don't startle, assuming it's our friendly guard coming to share an update on the random explosions causing chaos around us.

But I couldn't be any more wrong when I hear the voice of Dravin—Parla's partner and second in command. "Wren?" His voice is soft, calculated, and slightly comforting.

He's always been the more rational of the two. Which isn't exactly saying much considering Parla is a fucking lunatic dressed in pressed pantsuits.

I stand, my body going stiff as he enters my confinement.

He glances around, his gaze finally settling on me. Extending his hand, he says, "This is unacceptable. Come with me."

I stay firmly rooted in place. "What is this about?" I study his lazy posture and unkempt beard, the wisps of white giving away his older age.

"Our Furla Ain being held in a place like this is unspeakable." He motions once more. "Come."

With my arms crossed over my chest, I step toward him.

"Wren," Wes speaks through the grated barrier. "Don't fall for it. You're smarter than them."

I don't dare respond, because I don't want to give Dravin any more ammunition than he already has. Whatever he's up to, I will play along.

Dravin's expression softens when I approach, and he opens the door a bit further for both of us to fit through it. "This way, Ms. Oliver."

When I step into the hallway, the kind guard and I exchange a quick glance, but don't allow it to linger more than a second. I avert my gaze and walk alongside Dravin, past Wes's chamber and that of his other cellmates. I count the doors, making note of the locks on each of them and how far it takes to get from one end to the other. It's the little details that matter, the stuff people don't usually pay attention to. We round the corner and we're greeted by two more guards wearing standard-issue outfits, making them almost impossible to tell apart with their matching haircuts and arrogant demeanor. On a bad day, I could take down both of them, but it's the mystery lurking behind every corner that has me hesitant from acting just yet.

There's no telling how many more of them there are and the number of locks that stand in the way of our freedom.

"In here." Dravin places his hand on the small of my back and guides me to an open room.

I cringe at his touch and move to get away from him. The aroma is the first thing I notice, followed by the sight of fresh bread and large chunks of cheese sitting beside a steaming bowl of stew.

"You must be famished." Dravin strolls over and pulls out a chair from the small table and motions for me to sit.

I drag the thing from his grasp and scoot it in myself. "I've been hungrier."

Dravin strides over to the other side of the table, running his finger along the surface of it as he goes. He pulls out the only other chair and takes a seat. "May I?" He points to the chilled pitcher of water and nods toward the cup in front of me.

I eye him suspiciously and snatch the empty cup before he can pour anything in. I examine the inside, not seeing anything hidden within.

He chuckles. "I'd expect nothing less from you."

If they were going to poison me, they would have done it in the stew or various sides. I wouldn't so easily fall for the unsuspecting drink trick. I set the cup down, nudging it toward him in approval of his request, then turn my attention to the spread before me. They're probably assuming I would think they spiked my food, so it's possible they put the drugs in his, hoping I would swap the two. Meaning mine would be fine and his wouldn't be. But if they anticipated correctly, they might have guessed I'd do that, leaving the tainted food to actually be my own.

"What can I do to prove to you that the food is safe

to eat?" Dravin sips his own drink and leans back in his chair.

"You could start by taking these off." I hold my hands up where the cuffs still remain on my wrists, suppressing any power that lingers inside of me.

"You know I can't do that."

"Can't or won't?" I raise a brow despite already knowing the answer.

Dravin picks up his spoon and points it at my bowl. "Eat, we have much to discuss, no sense of doing it on an empty stomach."

I let out a chuckle and reach for the glass he poured for me. "Right." I sip the cool liquid and revel in the satisfaction of tasting something so fresh. When his eyes are trained on something other than me, I cautiously steal glances around the room, desperately searching for anything that could prove useful in my future plan; I pray to a higher power that one will come to me.

"Fine, suit yourself." He breaks off a hunk of bread and raises it toward his mouth.

"Give me that," I interrupt him from continuing.

He blinks a few times as if processing the request. Latching onto the piece he had set back on the table, he holds it out to me.

I shake my head and nod to the one still in his grasp. "That one."

Dravin rolls his eyes and sighs, tossing the bread over to me. "Let me guess, you'd like my stew, too?"

Considering he hasn't taken a single bite of it yet, I'll pass on finding out the hard way if it was poisoned. As much as I'd love to chow down on every last bit of this food, it's not worth the risk. "Have at it." I push my own bowl toward him. My mouth nearly waters at the sight of the cheese, but I settle on the bit of bread I'm semi-certain is safe to consume.

I nibble at the edge and take my time with the bread. Guilt floats in and reminds me of Wes's and Franny's poor conditions. The only food we've been given has been stale leftovers that were barely edible, and no doubt tainted in one way or another. I only allow myself the pleasure of the bread as a means to gain any kind of strength in hopes of breaking out of here. Without Wes's healing powers, it's up to my own body to fend for itself. I've made it this many years on my own, what's a little longer?

"What do you want to talk about?" I grow impatient with the game he seems to be playing.

Dravin pats the corners of his mouth with his napkin. "Well. I do have quite a few questions. Curiosity really, and a few formalities."

"Like?" I bite off some of the bread and chew it slowly.

"Perhaps we should start at the beginning, where everything seems to get blurry."

"You mean when you and Parla groomed me to be a demon assassin and used my anger as a tool?"

Dravin feigns surprise. "If I'm remembering

correctly, you came to us. You sought out our training programs, our expertise."

"I was a child." I slam my fist into the table.

Dravin flits his gaze behind me and lifts his hand to dismiss whoever is no doubt standing in wait to strike at a moment's notice. "We have many young recruits; you were no exception to that. You just happened to be the most gifted of them all."

"You used me."

He runs his hand through his beard. "I can see how you'd think that."

I narrow my gaze at him. "Think it? You're going to pretend it's not the truth? That your army isn't made up of orphaned kids who are full of rage and an insatiable hunger for revenge?"

"If that's what you choose to believe, there's no convincing you otherwise. You are a rather strong-willed woman."

I let out a quick and humorless laugh. "And that's the problem, now, isn't it? I'm no longer bending to your will, and that's become an issue for you." I circle my finger in the air. "And that's why you've locked me in here, because I'm not an asset anymore, I'm a fucking liability."

"Oh, Ms. Oliver, that is where you are mistaken. You are very much still an asset to our cause."

"Cause? Seriously? What the fuck does that even mean? What good could you possibly think you're doing here? Your main focus is to eradicate anyone who isn't like you. How are you okay with that?"

Dravin plops his elbow on the table and rests his head in his hand. "You're aware that not too long ago, you were fully supportive of our mission."

"Well, I changed my fucking mind."

"I see." He pauses briefly. "And that explains why instead of eliminating the target, you spread your legs to him instead."

"Are you fucking serious? *That's* what you think this is about?" I grit my teeth. "You think that lowly of me?"

"What else am I supposed to believe when our top hunter suddenly goes AWOL? Feel free to fill in the gaps for me if there's another version of the story."

"I almost died." The memory of that day comes floating in—flashes of the fight, locking eyes with Wes, not having any clue what the rattling in my chest was, and then being attacked and left for dead. "If it weren't for my *target*, I would have perished."

"So, one demon shows you the smallest kindness and you disregard everything you've worked toward your entire life?"

I open my mouth to speak, but I realize what he's doing. He's baiting me into admitting there are others. I'm playing right into his hand and if I'm not careful, I'll give away more than I should. "Maybe we could discuss that mission itself, how I was told it was routine, nothing out of the ordinary. You failed to mention it would be a challenge."

"I never once doubted your abilities, why put that in your head if it weren't necessary?"

"Are you missing the part where I almost died? Perhaps if I were better informed, none of this would have happened at all." Although, I'm glad everything has played out the way it has. Without this entire chain of events, I wouldn't have snapped out of my sheep-like mentality.

"And here you are, very much alive. It appears everything worked out the way it should have." Dravin brings his glass to his mouth and swallows some of the water before continuing. "We can fix this; get you back on track." He shifts his gaze around the room. "It doesn't have to be like this."

"Even if I were to agree, you know damn well that isn't true." I shake my head. "Parla would never allow that to happen."

"Perhaps if you provided her with some information, she'd be willing to forgive you of your wrongdoings."

I laugh again. "You're not serious, are you? You're as delusional as she is, as I once was. She's a monster, there's no convincing her of anything."

"I'll do everything in my power to prove you wrong." Dravin leans forward in his chair. "Tell me who you're working with."

I mimic his movement and narrow my gaze at him. "I don't know what you're talking about." The honest fucking truth. Parla was going on about some kind of spell blocking the extraction process, and I couldn't have been any more lost at what the hell she was talking about.

The only witches I've dealt with in the last few years have been those to spell my safehouses and maintain the integrity of keeping them concealed from both demons and hunters alike. My privacy has always been a priority and recent events have clarified the importance of that.

"You're making this harder than it has to be." Dravin plops a cube of cheese into his mouth and that alone makes me want to stab him in the throat with the spoon only inches away from my hand. "She won't stop until she gets what she wants. You're better off to just give in and forego whatever torture she has in store for you."

"Is that supposed to rattle me? To scare me into submission? There isn't a single thing either of you could do to me to make me help you ever again. I'd rather fucking die." I shove the rest of the bread into my mouth and savor the lingering warmth still locked within its tender insides.

"We don't want that to happen, Wren, none of us do."

I glare at him. "Because I'm too valuable, not because you care."

"You have this all wrong."

I reach for my cup, washing down the minimal substance I felt comfortable enough to consume.

Standing, I set the cup down with force, the bit of water remaining sloshes over the sides. "No, you do. You're a fool if you think I'd ever make this easy for you. You want answers? Why don't you give me some? What's the end game here? What's *really* going on? You use the story of war to disguise the hidden agenda. You create fear to propagate the compliance of everyone involved, keeping us in the dark about the bigger picture."

Dravin steadies his gaze between me and whoever is behind me.

"Are you fucking done with this good cop/bad cop charade?" I shove the offering he had tried to win me over with toward him, spilling the contents all over the table. "I will not be a puppet any longer!" I yell at him.

A shadow approaches from behind but I anticipate it coming from a mile away.

Fucking amateurs.

I shove the blunt end of the handle of the spoon right into the attacker's eye socket, twisting it and yanking it free.

The man screams and reaches for his face, giving me the perfect opportunity to place my hands around his head and snap his neck. His body falls to the floor with a thud and another man just like him appears.

I duck to block his blow and kick at his legs, knocking them out from under him and sending him next to his fallen comrade. "This isn't personal," I tell him knowing it wasn't too long ago that I was just like him, a soldier doing whatever I was told. It's not his fault that he's ignorant to the truth. Still, I cannot allow him to live, not when his very existence threatens my chance of ever getting out of here.

"Fucking bitch," he mutters while trying to regain his footing.

I slam my fist into his face and straddle his chest, pinning him to the ground and landing blow after blow across his face.

His nose cracks and sends blood trickling down and into his mouth. It splatters onto my face, misting me like a ripened orange does when you break it open. He tries to wrangle free of me but is too surprised by my overpowering that he can't seem to find a way to buck me.

A sharp clicking of heels threatens to steal my focus. Parla's annoying voice follows. "Wren Oliver, you have been charged with aiding and abetting a criminal of the highest caliber. With attacking and killing our kind, and numerous other offenses. You are sentenced to live out your days in Rock Bridge, pending parole, given your cooperation."

I continue to hit this man. "I. Will. Not. Cooperate. With. You." Each word is another fist to his blood-soaked and swollen face. I don't even realize that he's stopped moving until something sharp is jabbed into my neck. "I will get out of here. You fucking watch."

An explosion rattles the building and small pieces of debris float down from the ceiling.

"We'll get answers out of you one way or another."

And as the crippling realization that I've lost control consumes me, I'm taken under by whatever they injected into my veins.

Once again, making me believe that the end is finally near.

12
WREN

My arms ache from the restraints holding them in place.

I draw in a breath and lift my heavy head. My eyes fight to open, but when they do, I wish they hadn't after all.

Wes. Standing in the center of the room with chains around his wrists and ankles securing him to the concrete floor. His tired gaze meets mine, and it's like a thousand knives take turns slicing through my heart.

Franny was right, death would be coming soon. And here I am, staring it in the face.

"Oh, good, you're awake." Parla approaches from the side, stopping a few feet away. She crosses her arms over her chest and juts out her hip. All attitude, all the time. She glares over her left shoulder and then nods toward me.

"Wait," I call out, unsure what the fuck I plan on

saying next. Maybe if I stall them enough, *something* will happen. Perhaps a fucking miracle from the universe.

She blinks at me, clearly annoyed with having uttered a single word. "What?"

I look at Wes, and back at her. "Why are you doing this?" I take note of the rest of the room I can make out without being too obvious. Rollo, the old man who showed me kindness is avoiding us all and fiddling with his magical devices. A guard stands behind him, and there are at least two more posted up by the door.

Parla taps her pointed shoe against the floor. "You wouldn't understand."

"Enlighten me." Anything to prolong the inevitable while I run possible scenarios through my head. There has to be *something* we can do to get out of here. I gently tug at my wrists and grow weary of ever escaping the restraints. Wes seems impossibly bound, too, making this whole thing that much more difficult.

"I'm rather ambitious."

I study her otherwise beautiful face, noting the hard lines on her jaw and the sharp slope of her nose. I catch a slight twitch of her lip, like she's not quite being truthful. "And?"

Wes clears his throat. "Who hurt you?"

She rolls her eyes, but that alone is a giveaway that he struck a nerve. "No one."

"It was a demon, wasn't it?" He grips the chains and repositions his footing to focus on her.

Parla steps closer to me. "You think you love him, don't you? That he's in love with you?" She shakes her head. "They're incapable of such, and you know damn well it won't end well. I'm doing you a favor, Ms. Oliver. The sooner you're cut from his compulsion, the better. Although..." She swipes my hair off my shoulder and skims her fingers over the mark left behind by Bo. "There's no escaping that one. You're better off dead."

I shrug and try to evade her touch but it's nearly impossible tied to this chair. "You don't know what you're talking about. *One* of them hurt you, that doesn't make them all bad. That doesn't justify eradicating their whole species from our realm."

She dryly laughs. "Oh, you think I'm going to stop there?"

I process the severity of her statement. "You can't do that."

"Watch me." Her cheeks turn up into a devilish grin. "And you will help me do it."

"You're out of your mind."

"You have no choice." She pauses and looks me up and down. "You are making it rather difficult with that spell we can't seem to crack. But don't worry, we will break you one way or another."

"Why me? Why not another one of your many minions?"

"That is the ultimate question, isn't it?" She lets out a breath. "Must be tied to your lineage, but you're only one of the few who can actually survive after consuming a demon's essence. Most can only do a few months of it and then their weak little souls give out. You've been doing it since you came to us and we've been harvesting that power from you in batches, well, until a little over a year ago. That must have been when you found a witch to block us."

"You're giving me far more credit than I deserve. I didn't have a witch do anything to me."

Parla tips my chin up to look at her. "There's no sense in lying, we will figure it out."

But if what she's saying is true, why have they, all of a sudden, lost access to the demon energy remaining inside of me? I truly never have had a witch put a spell in place, so it had to have been done without my consent. Not that I'm upset about that, I'd just like to know what the hell is going on. Maybe if whoever did that would have told me back then what was happening, it would have saved me all this torment now.

"Why do you need all that power anyway, what do you plan on doing with it? Clearly, you don't *only* care about killing them; you want their energy, too."

"You are a curious little shit, aren't you?"

"If you're going to kill me, what's the harm in telling me what I'm going to die for?"

"Oh sweetheart, I have no intentions of ending your life. You're far too valuable to me alive." Her eyes bore into mine in a way that sends a chill down my spine. "But if you must know. The goal was always to reopen the borders."

My mouth falls open slightly. "What? I thought..."

She smirks and nods. "Because that's what we want you to think. That we're the reason it's in place. Otherwise, if our population believed it wasn't us, chaos would ensue. We keep the peace this way."

"The peace?" I laugh. "Having every single citizen afraid of the other is what you call peace? Pitting us against one another and justifying all the violence, and for what, your broken heart? News flash, *sweetheart*, you're not that important. People are betrayed every single day and they don't start wars over it.

"Do you not care about anyone other than yourself?" I nod toward Rollo, who appears to be practically crawling inside his own skin trying to escape this place. "Witches aren't even demons. What could he have possibly done to deserve this?"

"I don't have to explain myself to you." She motions to Rollo. "Now."

"You were fine with it a second ago, but now that I've struck a nerve you're done. It's almost like you *know* what you're doing is fucking wrong." I crane my neck to face the guards at the door. "Don't you see what she's making you do? This is *wrong*."

Parla grips my chin and yanks my head back around. "The demons and their bringers are the evil of this world, and they must be purged."

The same mantra I have told myself time and time again to justify all the killing I've done. There was a small part of me that felt it was wrong, but I clung to the image of my dead mother and childhood home burning to the ground to fuel the hatred I had for them. I slaughtered countless demons who were only trying to survive this hell that they were trapped into with no chance of escaping.

I suck in a breath and spit onto her polished and prim face. "Fuck you." I yank at the restraints around my wrists and block out the pain of my skin being torn under the pressure. My gaze meets Wes's, frantically hoping that his beast side will surface. "You have to do something, please."

He slowly shakes his head. "This is the only way."

"You can't possibly believe that." My heart shatters at seeing the defeat lining his features. How have they been able to break this unbreakable man?

Rollo kneels at my side. "I'm sorry," he whispers.

"No, whatever you're about to do, don't do it. You don't have to do it. I'll do anything else, just let him go."

Parla firmly grasps Rollo's shoulder. "Continue or I will find someone else to replace you." She trails her eyes from him to stare into mine. "First, you will end your boyfriend, and then, when the one who marked you comes for you, because there's no doubt in my mind that he will, you will kill him, too. And with that beacon on your neck finally fully engaged, you will become a magnet for every single creature left here in Prania. Once you have eliminated them all and I have broken the barrier, that's when the real fun will begin."

Rollo mutters an incantation and lightly holds onto

my hand. Something flickers in my chest and no matter how hard I fight it, I feel him enter my core. He takes Parla's hand in his other one and I watch in horror as whatever evil plan she has in place unfolds before me.

"It's done," he says while standing and averting his gaze to the floor. He steps away and returns to his place in the corner of the room.

"Wiggle your right foot," Parla tells me.

I comply without a thought, moving the thing to and from.

"Okay, now your left hand."

I do as she commands, my stomach turning at the loss of control over my body.

An explosion shakes our room, this one sounding the closest of all the rest. I will whoever is causing that chaos to plant one in here and kill each one of us before Parla can possibly get her way. I'd rather be dead than give this bitch any more power than she's already stolen.

"Guard, her restraints." She turns her attention to me. "You will not move unless I tell you to."

Despite my internal struggle, I nod in agreement.

The young man unlocks the cuffs on both my ankles and my wrists, leaving me free to escape and snap each one of their necks. But no matter how hard I try, I cannot bring myself to act on my desires.

"Stand."

I rise to my feet. "Please, don't do this."

"Approach the demon."

My body betrays me, stepping closer to this man who I share a fated bond with.

"It's okay," he whispers. "Don't fight it. You must do as she says. You get to live this way."

"I don't want to live without you." My voice cracks alongside my heart with each spoken word.

"I'll always be with you." Wes sighs. "I'll be in the sun that warms your skin on a bright day; in that bite of cheese that you savor because it's your last; I'll meet you in your dreams and maybe then I can give you the life you deserved; I'll be the partner I never got to be in this lifetime. And when it's finally your time to cross over, I will find you in the next life. I will always find you; I promise."

Tears well in my eyes. "Why didn't it work?"

Wes raises his upper lip to expose his fangs. They glisten under the fluorescent lighting.

I lower my voice even quieter than it already was. "You have to mark me?"

He nods, shifting his focus to the bitch behind me who is whispering to either the guard or Rollo, I can't be sure from this angle.

"Mark me, Wes. Please, I'm begging you. Fucking do it."

Wes grips the chains holding him in place. "I can't. And even if I could, there's no telling if it would work. If I would be able to save you. If you comply, you'll live, that's the only thing I'm sure of, Wren. You have to do whatever she tells you to."

I shake my head. "No, I won't do it." I speak louder. "Can I hug him, please? Give me that, Parla. If you understand the loss of love at all, you'll at least let me say goodbye."

"I don't owe you a damn thing." She approaches my side and places a small but deadly dagger in my hands. "You will do nothing but what I command you, do you hear me?"

My mind urges me to drive the thing into her cold heart, but my body won't allow it. Here stand the two most powerful beings in this whole prison, both completely unable to access their powers.

"It's okay," Wes reassures me again. "I will love you either way."

I study the delicate yet rugged features of his face, the thickness of his brows, and the ever so gentle curve of his lashes. Lips that I've kissed far too few times, and eyes that I wish would glow as they stare into mine.

Where has his beast side gone and why has it chosen to abandon us? I thought he loved me, cared for me, wanted me. But all I can see is that he left me and Wes here when we needed him the most. Why convince me to secure the bond but leave out one major fucking detail?

"Parla, please." I plead with her one last time.

"Kill the monster."

I inch closer to Wes, the dagger poised between us, aimed at his chest. "I can't stop it..." Uncontrollable tears stream down my cheeks, but they're mine, not some creation of Parla's command.

Wes doesn't move back, he doesn't try to avoid the inevitable. He embraces it like a long-awaited hug from a loved one. He lowers his arms to the side, allowing me to advance on him with nothing getting in the way. His body softens in anticipation of the end. "I will find you."

"You promise?" I continue forward despite conjuring every ounce of strength I have to withstand her authority.

"With all my heart." Wes blinks and for a split second, there's a flicker of red that ignites in his eyes, but as quick as it appears, it's gone again.

Could the mate bond be in place enough that he's telling the truth? I'll never know, but I accept the comfort that I will see him eventually, one way or another. We will get our happily ever after in a different life.

Something stirs inside of me, but I'm afraid it might not be strong enough to overpower Parla. "I'm sorry." I collapse into him, shoving the weight of the dagger forward.

Parla triumphantly gasps from behind me, but I refuse to let her win that easily.

"Now, Wes!"

Without wasting a single precious fucking moment, his fangs pierce the flesh on the side of my neck. Pain and pleasure ignite under my skin and my eyes nearly roll back in my skull.

Wes's arms do what they can to hold me upright despite the chains hindering him from having a full range of motion. His moans vibrate my tender skin, and his touch warms my body.

Mark him, a voice rings through my mind. *Do it*, it calls out louder.

"Kill him," Parla screams at me.

But one of the commands is stronger than the other, so I comply, biting into the exposed part of his shoulder closest to me.

Wes tenses and groans, his temperature rising to the point it becomes painful to be this near him. But no amount of torment could be worse than killing my fated mate.

Blood pools in my mouth and I swallow the coppery liquid down. Once I'm certain I've done what I was supposed to do, I break away and meet his gaze.

His shock and surprise match mine, but I'm riddled with fear that I have done something terribly wrong. That this isn't what he wanted. I asked him to mark me, but he never asked me to mark him. I've done this against his will and what if he never forgives me for this blatant disregard for his autonomy.

Through clenched teeth, Wes mutters, "Get back."

"I'm sorry." A drop of his blood rolls down my chin. "I'm so sorry."

"I said *kill him*," Parla yells once more.

I turn on my heel, regaining control over my body

with each movement. "No, you said to kill the monster." I twirl the blade in my grasp. "And the way I see it, you're the only one of those in this room."

Parla's eyes widen in horror at the sight before her.

The trained assassin she betrayed, stalking toward her with the knife she so foolishly gave.

"Do something!" She clumsily steps back and shakes Rollo. "Guards!"

As much as I want to slit her throat right now and get it over with, there's still the matter of Wes being tied to the chamber floor. I refuse to allow her to command these pathetic excuses for men to end his life while I'm distracted with her.

But to my continued surprise, Wes is no longer in the condition he was only seconds prior. No, his entire body burns red hot, flames attempting to flicker along his skin.

"Get back," he grunts again, his voice strained. "I don't want to hurt you."

A low and throaty rumble sounds from deep within him, and it's enough to cause Parla's minions to hesitate in advancing him. They're no doubt just as uncertain of what's about to happen as we all are.

"What are you waiting for?" she yells at them once more.

Two almost identical looking men spare a glance at each other and then advance. I shouldn't discard my only weapon, but without thinking twice, I reel my arm into position and send the blade soaring across the room and through the chest of the one closest to Wes.

Wes roars and I can't quite tell if he's in pain or simply frustrated. He wraps his burning hands around the chains attached to the floor and pulls with all his might. The concrete where the thing is anchored buckles but doesn't give yet.

Three more soldiers run into the room and that's when I fully comprehend how outnumbered we are in this place.

Will that stop me from fighting to the death? Absolutely-fucking-not.

I take off into a sprint toward them, sliding to the floor at the last second and knocking one of them onto the ground. I fumble with the knife tucked into his waistband and drag it out, shoving it rapidly into his torso. One down, many more to go.

Adrenaline pumps through my veins and for the first time in a long while, I feel right at fucking home.

A random guard latches onto the back of my head, snatching me by the hair and yanking me off his lifeless comrade. "Fucking bitch." He kicks me in the side and pulls his foot up to stomp on my head.

Little does he know, I've been in this position countless times before, and his carelessness is no match for my cunning. With the handle of the knife still poised in my grasp, I roll out from under his attack and drive the sharp end into his thigh, grinding it in place and fully fucking enjoying the sheer terror that devours him.

"Who's the bitch now?" I slide the blade out and rise to my feet. Grabbing a fistful of his hair, I tug his head back and make a clean cut straight across his neck.

Blood splatters onto my face and I smile as I shove him onto the floor to finish bleeding out. I skim my gaze over the men standing in wait, their natural instincts causing them to consider whether this battle is worth dying for. "Who's next?"

"Enough," a familiar voice calls out from behind me.

Dravin.

Over my shoulder I catch him muttering something to Parla.

Wes, still struggling with whatever transition he's going through, burns hotter with each passing second. The temperature of the room rises along with him, and I consider how much longer we can stay in here at this rate.

"What are you waiting for?" Parla screams at the men. "You're telling me you can't take down *one* girl?"

As if coming to a collective decision, they advance on me. I try to count them, but I lose track after seven blurred figures charge at me. I smirk, ready to accept my fate either way.

I swipe the blade through the air, hoping to make contact in some capacity. I duck to avoid a fist as I'm met with another kick to the chest. I grab onto the foot and circle, creating a diversion from the brunt of the attacks. I send that man into the throng of other men and get hit from behind with a violent burst of air. "What the fuck?" I blurt out through my ragged breath.

Parla's hand remains extended while the other is latched onto Rollo tightly while he mumbles something beside her. She's channeling his magic to try to win this fight. And if I'm not careful, she very well could.

It's one thing for her to use her pathetic soldiers and her own weak attempts to subdue me, but I'm no match to old magic. I could easily cast a knife through the air and end Rollo, eliminating her assistance, but despite him aiding in my torture, I know he's only doing it to save his own life. I can't fault him for trying to stay alive. Especially when he has shown moments of benevolence to me when given the opportunity.

A laugh bubbles out of my chest. "You're too much of a coward to fight your own battles."

She slams another burst of power into my chest, knocking me off-kilter and rattling my core. She rapid fires two more, then follows it up with some kind of paralytic magic, rendering me incapable of moving a single inch. "Your strength," she spits through her teeth. "Is only because of me. Don't you dare for a second question that."

The heat in the room rises.

She flits her attention toward Wes briefly and then

to the men behind me. "Subdue her." When they hesitate, she adds, "Now!"

Dravin raises his hand to put them at ease. "I'll do it." He strolls across the room and pauses at my side. "Cuffs?" he asks a guard. Dravin kneels, his gaze meeting mine. "This could have been easy, Wren, but you always have to make things difficult." His clammy hand reaches out to grasp mine, securing the restraint on one of my wrists.

I inhale deeply, my jaw clenched tightly. My stare flicks to Parla, and then Dravin. I meet Wes's painfully fiery gaze and consider all the things we both could have done differently to end up anywhere but here.

"In another life," I whisper.

"What's that?" Dravin questions.

A sensation I've felt before flutters in my chest. Not from when I first saw Wes, but on another occasion. A quiet rumble starts low in my core, and rises to the top, like water shifting from a simmer to a soft boil. Only the more heat that it's exposed to, the greater the intensity it will become, spilling over the sides if not careful.

I wiggle my pinky, grateful for the smallest ounce of control it gifts me. But will it be enough when I'm this close to being bridled once again?

Dravin secures the other cuff in place, my heart dropping in response to the realization that this is all about to end and there will be nothing I can do to stop it. "It's better this way."

Wes roars loudly, garnering the attention of every

remaining member alive in the room. He clutches his chains and pulls them straight from their concrete securement with minimal effort. With his legs still attached, he reaches to the nearest guard, latching onto him and dragging him toward him like a child's doll. The man's standard-issued uniform melts away at Wes's touch and he lets out a shrieking scream when his skin bubbles from the flame melting away his flesh. Wes sinks his mouth into the man's neck and rips his throat out, spitting it onto the floor and tossing the body aside. He grasps for more life forces to end but comes up short, another ear-shattering howl escaping him.

"There you are," I speak softly.

"Not happening," Parla cries. "Rollo, do something."

But as if he finally refuses to continue to aid her in this despicable act, he wiggles free of her hold and swipes a vial off the table. He pulls the cork, discarding it onto the floor without a care, and tips the thing back, swallowing the contents in one gulp. "No." He shakes his head and meets my gaze. "I'm sorry."

I struggle against the hold still keeping me in place, slowly breaking through it. A memory suddenly floats into my mind; Dash being held in place, his neck snapped in front of me, wishing like hell I could have reached him in time. I had caught his body as he collapsed to the ground, and my heart ripped apart knowing there was nothing I could do to bring him back to life. Our only saving grace was the fact that

Dash's powers surfaced, gifting us with his life from his ashes.

But now, watching this man with thick wrinkles and endless gray hair, I know I couldn't possibly be that lucky twice in one lifetime.

He may not mean to me what Dash does, but it's still a life that doesn't deserve to die, especially not like this.

His shaking form hits the floor and Parla clutches her chest, her sights quickly moving from him to me.

I move faster than I ever have in my life and wrap the new chained cuffs on my wrists around Dravin's throat, using the weight of my body to fall back and pull with everything I can. My only regret is that I won't see the life leave his eyes when I end him for good. My trade-off is that I get to witness Parla's eyes nearly pop out of their sockets at her partner being murdered by the *girl* she thought she could screw over.

"You're next," I call out to her while waiting for Dravin to stop squirming under my authority.

She runs past me, shoving any guard she can toward us. "Do not let them escape."

An explosion shakes the walls and I have to press my eyes shut to protect them from the debris that flutters down from the ceiling.

When I open them, not only is she gone, but Wes is, too. His entire body is covered by guards attacking him in every direction. The fear I felt when I lost Dash floods through me and I can't get Dravin's heavy corpse off of me quick enough. I wiggle out from under him and shove his body aside, gasping for breath now that I'm free of his weight.

"Wes!" I scream through troubled lungfuls of air. Locating the first weapon I can find, I snatch an arm's length dagger from the man Wes had ripped apart. I latch onto one of Wes's attackers but instead of killing him swiftly, he pushes me and knocks me to the ground.

His face is lined with dread and his damp skin is ashy and pale. Instead of pursuing me, he takes off into a sprint out of the room, leaving us all behind.

I guess that's one way to eliminate the enemy. But it's also possible he's going to call in reinforcements, and there are only so many people I can take on at once.

Pressing my palm into the floor, I try to regain my footing again, my wrist aching under the pressure. It nearly gives out, but I grit through the pain and refuse to let it keep me down. "Wes," I cry into the crowd again.

The sound of knives slicing through flesh fills the space, along with grunts and groans caused by who fucking knows. Each moment that passes, I grow more concerned with the condition in which I will find him in after I kill every last one of these men.

Sweat beads on my forehead and trickles along my spine with the continued increase in temperature.

A roar so loud it rattles the chamber the same way the explosion had done earlier fills the space. I take pause, my heart pounding wildly in suspense for whatever will follow.

In a burst of red, the men surrounding Wes scatter, some of them quite literally flying through the air and slamming into the walls. One body slams into mine, knocking me down for what seems like the millionth time.

I stare in disbelief as Wes emerges from the chaos, his entire body a mixture of fire and smoke. His arms contort and he lets out a bellowing howl, his chin tilting toward the ceiling like he's in immense pain. I blink and his frame twists in an unnatural manner. I blink again and he's down on all fours, gasping for air and shoving his fist into the floor.

What is happening to him? Is all of this because I asked him to mark me? Because I marked him without his consent? What have I done?

I get my footing while I glance around at the fallen bodies, some whimpering and some completely still. None of them are a threat to us anymore—not in their condition. That's not to say more of them won't appear, though.

Our chance has finally come, and we need to act now if we intend on getting out of here. Parla escaped but there's no doubt in my mind that she's rallying every ounce of back-up she can to ensure we never leave this place.

I turn my focus back to Wes, but I struggle to make sense of what my sights have locked on. Black fur covers his face and lines the sides of his neck, claws protrude from his fingertips, and his hindquarters have...

I shake my head. *No, this can't be right.* I must have fallen hard and got knocked out.

But the more I stare, the more my disbelief evolves into complete and utter shock.

It's not until the man I'm fated to is no longer a man at all. He's a creature, standing on all fours, and yet he's nearly as tall as me, with onyx fur and flames dancing over his sleek coat. The only similarity between the two is those familiar glowing red eyes that I've yet to grow tired of seeing. I've come across werewolves and shifters of varying kinds in all my days, but never one of this caliber.

The details of the last few weeks rise to the surface, all pointing to an outcome I never expected. His control over Bo, the alpha of alphas. The occasions when the guys would slip up and mention the term *hound*. His sheer strength and almost impossibly rare brute force. The reason Parla was so fucking determined to get me to consume his essence, because it would be the most potent one in this realm —giving her immense power to do whatever she wished.

Wes is no man, he's a hellhound.

A myth to this world that I never imagined could be real.

Saliva drips from his exposed fangs and he slowly

takes a step forward, the way a predator does before attacking their prey.

I place both hands in the air between us. "Wes, it's me."

I should be afraid, perhaps even run, but if this is what fate has decided, who am I to alter our course?

13

WES

This has never happened to me.

None of it.

Not the immense pain, not the tethering between two forms, not the complete and total shift into my beast side.

I didn't even know it was possible.

I thought that was a myth—something made up in old fables that were an exaggeration of the truth. Some nighttime story told to children to lull them to sleep and ensure they stayed put in their beds.

But when every single bone in my body cracked and moved around, rearranging into something entirely different than I've been all my life, I knew.

I fucking told you, that arrogant voice in my head calls out. *Now, give me control.*

Never. I fight back. Because there's no telling what he'll do if I give him the reins.

Hunger, unlike anything I've ever experienced, threatens to consume my entire focus. For what exactly, I'm not sure. A burger, a human heart, maybe a piece of chocolate cake. I don't know, but I want it all.

Then, take it all, my beast suggests.

I ignore him and blink through the lids of my shifted form. I try to take in my shape, noting the fur covering my hind legs and side. My entire being is thickly covered in a black coat. Saliva drips out of my gaping mouth and as strange as this new body is, it's oddly freeing. It's strong, nimble, and full of energy, both a blessing and curse, considering I want nothing more than to run around in circles and chase my fucking tail. What a strange thing to desire.

We have time.

No, we don't. I cautiously move forward like a baby taking its first steps.

"Wes, it's me," Wren says with her hands outstretched.

I open my mouth to speak to her, but it comes out as a growl. I guess being in my shifted form doesn't exactly offer the best communication. I get closer, only to find that my continued presence seems to induce the fearful look gracing her features. The exposed teeth, heavy breathing, and salivating mouth don't help the situation either. Not to mention, despite being on all fours, I'm nearly looking her in the eyes.

Still, I hope that she trusts me enough to continue. I lower my head, inching closer to her until the top of my scruff rests against her still extended hand. I brace myself, unsure if she will accept me in this form. It's one thing for her to want to be with me when I'm mainly a man, but now, I'm all hound.

There's nothing wrong with us, my hound snaps at me.

Then why are you just as nervous as I am?

Things were already complicated when a demon was fated to a hunter—I can't imagine what must be going through her mind as that demon she had only just grown to accept has shifted into a blasphemous creature.

Wren's cool fingers weave their way through my fur, melting the tension in my bones like a hot knife on butter. I nestle into her touch and she responds by wrapping her arms around the base of my neck and hugging me tightly.

"I thought you were going to fucking eat me," she laughs into my side.

My own laugh comes out like another muffled growl. I really have to stop trying to do normal human things in this form.

How do I shift back? I question my hound, because the realization that I have no idea how to control the transformation suddenly hits me.

So soon?

I'm distracted by his arrogance and completely miss the threat incoming from Wren's flank. A man reaches for her, yanking her free of me and sending her into the hard floor. I act, not even hesitating, by pouncing on him and pinning his shaking body to the concrete. I latch my mouth around his jaw and rip the bottom half of his skull off. I toss it aside, the metallic of his blood bursting my tastebuds to life. My hound takes over, clawing his chest, making damn sure there's no way he could ever recover from his wounds.

He was already dead, you idiot, I tell him.

Don't lie, you're enjoying this as much as I am.

He overpowers me once more and rushes to another whimpering guard, latching onto his torso and flipping him over. The guard lets out a yell, but it's no use, neither I nor my hound intend on allowing him to live. Not after he threatened Wren's life.

Time becomes this bizarre passing thing, and each moment is now counted by the lives we manage to end together. We take turns clawing and biting and devouring our prey. The only reason we stop is because the last remaining heartbeat in the room is our beloved.

"Wes!" she screams. "Are you fucking in there? We have to go."

I nod, but knowing how everything else I do seems to be lost in translation, I have no idea what this actually looks like on her end.

I need to shift back into my other form, hound.

But we're just getting started.

I crane my head around and latch onto my arm, biting it with enough pressure to cause both of us pain. I sense the lack of control slip for a brief moment.

"This way!" Wren motions while running out of the room. She dodges the incoming attack of a guard and drives a knife into his side, yanking it out and kicking him off his feet. She glances back to make sure I'm following her, not phased at all about the man she just killed so easily.

Because she is like us.

Finally, I agree with my other side.

Wren may be small, she might be dainty and beautiful as a flower, but she's poison wrapped in a deceiving package and she is my perfect match.

Wind caresses my fur as the three of us rush down the corridor and enter the hallway of chambers that have kept us captive for far too long.

Everest's gaze meets Wren's, then goes wide when he locks his sights on me. He fumbles at his side to retrieve a weapon. "Holy shit, behind you."

Wren rushes in front of me to block his path. "It's Wes, he won't hurt you." She looks over her shoulder. "Right, Wes?"

I expose my teeth on accident, not quite in control of all the mannerisms of a hound, yet. And I'm not entirely sure the beast side of me wasn't doing that for show. I pause in front of Tremont's door, sniffing around the thing and trying to find some way to open it. I claw at the thick metal exterior, penetrating it but not enough.

I need to shift, you fucking idiot. You're wasting time,

and if you ruin our chance of getting out of here, I'll lock you back in a cage for good.

A loud roar bellows up and out of my chest, followed by the crunching of bones. I scream as the pain settles into every inch of my body. Snapping, popping, cracking. Everything becomes a blur of red-hot scorching agony until I'm left in the fetal position, completely fucking naked and whining like a baby.

Get it together, it wasn't that bad.

My hound is a real asshole.

I blink a few times to adjust my eyes and get used to the newness of being in my original form. Cool hands hover along my skin once more, grounding me to the here and now. "Wren," I mutter.

"Are you okay?" Her steady blue gaze focuses on mine. "Here." She shoves the clothes I was once wearing on top of my exposed body. "I thought these might come in handy."

"Yeah," I croak. "Thanks." I slide the pants over my legs and toss the shirt over my head. I cup her cheek in my hand and skim my thumb along the soft edge of her skin. "We'll talk later, okay? When this is all over."

There are a million things I need to say to her, but they'll all have to wait. None of this will have mattered if we get caught again and lose the little bit of an advantage we've gained.

"Okay." Wren nods, standing up and extending her hand to me.

I latch onto it and she helps me to my feet. I wobble

slightly but regain my footing. I've spent my entire life with these two legs and somehow, they feel entirely foreign.

Because your true form is as a hound.

"Shut up," I accidentally say out loud. I grip Wren's shoulder. "Not you, I'm sorry." I point to my chest. "The idiot that lives in here."

An explosion rattles the walls of the building and causes the three of us to brace ourselves and cover our heads.

"What the fuck is going on out there?" I ask Everest.

He shrugs, "I'm not sure. They don't tell us much, only that we must protect the integrity of keeping our prisoners locked away."

My gaze trails to Wren's neck, where a fresh set of fang marks are now at home next to the ones that Bo had left on her. "Can you still feel him?" I reach out and skim the scar that remains from his marking.

Wren presses her hand against mine and sighs. "Yeah."

"Good." That means Bo is still alive. And given nothing has changed with Dash's supernatural abilities, he should be, too. For the first time since knowing both of them, I worry more for Bo's well-being than Dash's, considering Dash can resurrect if he dies. Bo is fierce and nearly unstoppable, but he's still capable of being killed. Being trapped in enemy territory only guarantees that will eventually happen if nothing changes.

Gripping the handle of Tremont's door, I tug the thing and pound on it with my other hand. "You in there?" I slam my fist against the metal exterior and it rattles in response.

"Wes, is that you?" The older man calls out.

"I'm going to get you out of there, and then we need to run." I turn toward Wren and Everest. "We need to free as many prisoners as we can."

Wren nods and rushes over to where Everest is standing and fumbling with his key-filled chain to find the one to open Wren's cellmate's chamber.

I hike my leg up on the exterior of Tremont's door and channel every ounce of strength I can muster. The heat along my skin rises, flames flickering to the surface and gracing me with their presence. To anyone else, the temperature would be unbearable, but to me, it's a familiar friend I welcome to my side.

"Come on!" I groan as the door bends to my strength. I yank the thing free from its hinges and pry it open enough to allow a person to slide through.

Catching my breath, I run my fingers through my hair to swipe it out of my face. "Tremont." I nod toward Wren and Everest. "Go with them." I flit my attention to my fated mate. "I have to find my people. I'll catch up with you soon enough, I promise."

"Wes," Wren calls out. "No." She reaches her arm out to me. "I just got you back." She rushes past the man I just freed. "I'll go with you."

I shake my head. "It's too dangerous. I need you to get them out. I'll find you."

Everest drops the keys onto the ground and frantically retrieves them. "I can't find the fucking master key."

The longer it takes for him to free this girl, the more danger Wren is put in.

I exhale a puff of smoke and take things into my own hands. I walk over to him, nudging him out of the way. "Keep looking for it." I repeat the same thing I had done on Tremont's cell, positioning my leg on the outside of the frame, and digging in deep to garner my strength. A guttural bellow escapes me and I fall back as the door gives way. "There. Now all of you, *out*." I look to Wren. "That includes you."

The whole fucking reason I allowed Wren to risk her life at all was to attempt to save my people—we can't be this close and I not try to find them. This can't be all for nothing. It's not until I'm a few feet away that I glance over my shoulder and catch sight of the person who appears from the shadows of their captivity.

I stop dead in my tracks, my heart pounding wildly. Slowly, I turn toward this girl with dark brownish red hair and a glistening stare. "It's you," I gasp, my mind not quite wrapping itself around the reality of seeing her face again.

"It's me." Tears well in her eyes and roll down her cheeks.

"You two know each other?" Wren points between the two of us.

"*You* two know each other?" The feisty red-head quips back, motioning to me and Wren.

I close the space between us in an instant, my arms wrapping around the small frame of this girl I thought I'd never find. I breathe her in and spin her in a circle before gently putting her back on her own feet. Gripping each of her shoulders, I look her over. "You're okay, you're really okay?" Aside from growing the hell up, she's otherwise unharmed. A small scar lines her brow and dirt speckles her body. Her clothes are tattered and aged, but it's nothing a long shower and a pint of ale won't remedy.

She shoves me hard in the chest and slaps me across the face. "What took you so long?"

My heart aches at knowing she's been here all along and I hadn't figured out how to break in and save her. "Blame your brother."

Her gaze shifts behind me as if she's looking for a ghost. "Is he? He's alive."

I reach for Wren, my arm lingering in the air waiting for her. "According to the mark on her neck."

Wren appears at my side, her fingers sliding around mine, and her other hand wrapping around my forearm. "You're Bo's sister?"

Tremont clears his throat. "Listen, I don't mean to break up this family reunion, but we should get going."

"Not by blood," Jade tells Wren. "But close enough." She glances over at Everest. "Are you coming with us?"

Everest steadies his gaze on her, like he's trying to make sure she's aware of just how serious the words that are about to come out of his mouth are. "I'm not going anywhere without you."

I ignore the brotherly instincts that arise and decide that's a battle I will wage another day. "Where's..." But before I can finish my question, Jade bows her head and rocks it back and forth.

"I'm sorry, Wes."

I swallow down the pain that rises and the guilt that follows. If I had only been smarter, more strategic, quicker—I could have saved her, too. Now, the only mother I've ever known is another casualty in this endless war.

I came to terms with the loss of her a million times over, but with the finality of it sinking into place, the wound rips open deeper than before.

Everest holds a key between his fingers carefully, like he's afraid he might lose it forever if he lets go.

"Is that the master?" I ask him.

He nods in confirmation.

I draw in a breath and squeeze Wren's hand. "How do we get out of here?"

Everest goes into strategy mode. "Sector twelve took the biggest hit. We're a few sectors over. If we can make it past whatever guards are still holding their ground, we have a clear shot out of here."

"How many are there?" I ask despite being afraid to know the answer.

"If you mean guards, there's no telling on any given day. Sectors though...there are eighteen." He points to the faint number painted on the wall, telling us that we're in the very last one.

I do the math quickly in my head and glance down the corridor. "Are we clear?"

"Yes, the other two prisoners were downgraded upon your arrival."

"We have six sectors to empty between here and freedom." I look at each one of the people around me. "Are you ready to fight?"

"I was born ready," Wren chimes in immediately, a grin forming on her beautiful face.

Tremont holds his cuffed hands in the air. "I'm not much help without my powers."

"Can you do anything about that?" I glance at Everest and then down the hall in anticipation for whatever army Parla is no doubt forming to stop us.

"Not yet, but if you broke out of the interrogation room and left behind any bodies, there should be something on one of them to get the cuffs off."

"Jade, stay close." I ruffle the hair on her head, falling into the routine of annoying her the way I had done in the past.

"I don't go by that anymore. Not since..."

The years aren't the only thing that has changed. She's older now, more mature, but more weathered, too. She's been through hell and that little girl who would run around picking wildflowers and insisting on making Bo and I jewelry out of them is no longer. Her innocence has been stripped and that's something that can never be replaced. It wasn't just me that lost a mother figure, it was her, too. And where I had Bo and Dash to fill that void, she had no one. She was left here all alone to eventually fall to the same fate that Mother did.

"What should I call you then?" I wrap my arm around her shoulder and pull her close.

She looks up at me, her eyes still red and watery. "Maybe I could get used to Jade again."

An explosion shakes the building, and we huddle together, the men shielding the women from the brunt of the debris that falls from the ceiling.

"I think they're hitting every sector!" Everest shouts over the echoing of the boom.

"There they are!" A man yells from the end of the hallway, which doubles as our only way out.

"Stay behind me," I tell them while stepping in front. Lowering my head, I let my powers rise to the surface, growing comfortable with that welcoming flicker of flame that nips at my skin.

14
WREN

I get as close to Wes as I can without getting burnt. "I'm only staying back here because I don't want you to set me on fire."

He stalks toward the guards, swatting away their pathetic attempts to subdue him with tranquilizers. He grips one of them by the throat and raises their body completely off the ground, no doubt crushing their windpipe and then tossing them aside. "Who's next?"

I grin and find a gap between him and the wall that I can squeeze through, readying the blade at my side and going to work at what I do best. *Fight.*

First, I was stolen by monsters, and now here I am, fighting for them.

I guess that's what happens when you fall in love with the enemy.

Wes acknowledges me by giving me some space to evade his heat.

The temperature really does grow rather rapidly in such tight quarters. Part of me wants to reach out and touch it. To embrace the fire that lives within him, but I know better than to think I could do it without consequence.

I drive my blade into a guard's leg, yanking it out and shoving it into the same man's neck. Blood spurts out and I move on to my next target, going through the motions like my body is running on autopilot. I duck an incoming blow, and then take another to the side, the wind escaping my lungs temporarily. I spin on my heel and push my next target off balance and into Wes's grasp.

He snaps his neck, burning the man's cheeks in the process. Wes wrings his hands to free himself of the dead guard's melted flesh.

I pause mid-plunge as I'm about to end another life, only to realize the guard I had latched onto is actually on our side. "Fucking hell, you're going to have to take that stupid fucking outfit off. I almost killed you."

I release him and glance around to the rest of them, counting the standing bodies and hoping we didn't suffer a loss.

A fallen man groans and Wes kneels beside him to finish him off.

"I'm Everest, by the way." He extends his hand toward me.

I wipe the blood of my victims on my leg and place my palm in his. "Sorry about that, Everest. I'm Wren."

He shrugs. "Honest mistake." Everest grips the center of his buttoned-up shirt and rips them to the side, the buttons popping off and littering the already messy floor, revealing a plain white tee underneath.

Franny, or well, Jade, helps him out of the sleeves and tosses the thing onto a dead man. They exchange a bashful glance like an innocent crush would.

"Interrogation room, then clearing out the sectors one at a time, moving as quickly as possible. Got it?" Wes stares at each of us, his gaze lingering on mine.

Watching him take control like this sends a rush straight to a place we don't have time to stop and rectify.

The second we get a chance to breathe, that's another story.

As if he recognizes the blaze that burns in my own stare, he hides a smirk and steps over a body, walking headfirst into the unknown.

"Can you fight at all?" I ask the old man just standing like a bump on a log, eyes wide and a bit terrified. I follow Wes's path and the rest take up the rear.

"With my magic, yes. I'm rather useless without it."

Wes simmers the fire burning on his exterior and glances over his shoulder at me.

I quicken my pace to catch up to him, comfort settling over me at being by his side. I've never been the type to fall in line behind a man and that isn't going to change just because my fated mate is some powerful and mighty creature. His authority and control are sexy, but there's a time and place for it, and it won't take away from everything I've built and earned on my own.

He keeps his voice low. "We're carrying the weight of three others, you're aware of that, right?"

I look up at him. "There will be casualties."

His gaze trails down my body and back up to meet mine. "Let me heal you, please."

I breathe in deeply and train my attention ahead of us. "I'm fine."

Truth is, no matter how skilled I am at fighting, Wes is still our best chance of making it out of here alive. He needs to be at one hundred percent, not just for himself, but for us, too. I refuse to weaken him and risk everything because of some minor injuries.

We step into the room where everything changed. The bodies of those Wes ripped to shreds still lie on the floor, their blood and innards soaking into the concrete.

"Rollo!" Tremont gasps and rushes over to the dead man.

I suppress my sorrow and rummage for anything that could be of use. I snatch a set of keys off a guard and hold them out to Everest. "Does this have a master, too?"

"Here." He gives the one in his hand to Fran—Jade —and looks the new one over. "It appears so."

I slide a knife from another dead body and tuck it into my waistband.

"These marks." Jade nudges a corpse with her shoe. "Are animalistic."

I continue to check for loot and ignore the secret that is not mine to share.

"About that..." Wes says after what feels like an eternity. "When we get out of here, we have a lot to discuss."

I observe Jade out of the corner of my eye, her brow raised at Wes.

"I'd say so." She lets out a long breath. "My brother marked a hunter, and you're fated to her."

"That's probably not the most surprising of it all."

"You're not going to tell me Dash is dead, are you? Because I've been avoiding asking this whole time, afraid you dropped the ball on him, too."

Another secret that isn't mine to confess.

I stand and grip her shoulder as I pass. "Dash is alive."

"I don't understand why he would do this..." Tremont stands from his spot near Rollo and wipes away a tear.

"Him," Everest points across the room. "That guy should have something to get those cuffs off."

Dravin.

"I've got this." Wes holds out his hand to stop me.

I don't protest because I'd rather not have to look at that bastard ever again if I can help it.

"He was kind to me," I tell Tremont. "Parla made him torture me. The first time, he attached this black pain device to my chest and I swear he compromised it because there was this burst of light and it quit working. She was using him to abuse me, and he refused to allow it to go on, that's why he took his own life." I point to the discarded vial he consumed. "He drank that before anyone could stop him."

Everest approaches with a small silver-looking rock. He reaches toward Tremont, taking one of his hands into his, and waves the thing over his cuff. It unlatches and falls to the floor with a clang.

Tremont gives him the other one and rubs at his wrists once they're finally free. "Thank you."

"How do you feel?" I study him carefully, wondering if he's going to turn and use his magic against us. My hand rests readily on the knife at my waist.

Tremont takes in his fallen friend and then those around us. "Like we need to get out of here."

"Two master keys?" I point to Everest and Jade.

They nod and hold them for us to see.

"You can rip the doors off the hinges." I flit from Wes over to Tremont. "We'll hold off any guards that come our way. Got it?"

Tremont turns his wrist over, a crackling of magic rising to the surface like he's manifesting electricity. "Got it."

A million uncertainties run through my mind but I push them all aside and focus on the few things I can control. Like getting us out of here alive.

"You'll want to hang onto this." Everest shoves the silver apparatus into Tremont's hand. "The demons will be cuffed, too."

I rush to the entrance of this room to join Wes at his side. "You ready for this?"

He stares back at me, his eyes glowing redder than I've ever seen before. "Let's get out of here."

A place that is known to be inescapable. A prison where demons go to rot, to be abused, to die. A one-way ticket to their demise, with no chance of ever seeing the light of day again. Only, they made a gigantic mistake thinking they could hold us captive without a fight. They may have held us for a little while against our will, but the time has come to unleash those they deem monsters.

We step into the smoke-filled corridor and I blink to adjust my eyes to the thickness of the air. Readying a knife in both of my fists, I walk at Wes's flank down the long windy hall. I count the footsteps behind me, noting the differences among them. Jade's and Everest's are almost in tandem, while Tremont's are staggered and hobbled like he has a slight limp.

I'm not entirely sold that we aren't making a mistake by allowing him to tag along, but what else were we supposed to do—leave him here?

We need every bit of help we can get if we want to make it out alive. Not just from this prison, but from this enemy territory we're trapped in. I'll be able to get us out using my hunter's mark, and then we'll be on the run for who knows how long until they catch up.

Parla will stop at nothing to make me pay for disrupting her evil plan and I have no doubt that she will spare no expense to track me down and suck the life out of me, along with every single demonic essence still lingering within my being.

"Incoming," Wes warns only a moment prior to my own senses kicking in.

"Sector seventeen," Everest adds from behind.

"Spread out." I motion for them to move out of the way. "Wes and I will take the lead. Tremont, you cover them. You two open whatever cells you can."

Wes claims the wall next to him, and I slide along the one at my side. I focus my breathing and channel my strength to carry me through. Each sector we clear is one step closer to our freedom. Something that was once so far out of reach, now taunting us with its proximity.

"Shh," a guard whispers to another. "I hear something."

"You're being fucking paranoid, Briggs. They escaped out of eighteen."

Little does he know, he's massively misinformed.

The two of us pop around the corner and grab each of them, Wes catching his victim on fire while I slit the throat of the other. It's cruel and inhumane, but we don't have the luxury of anything else.

"Get to work," I tell the others, eyeing the corridor

as far as I can see. I spare Wes a glance. "That was easy, too easy."

He tips his head. "You're right." Gripping onto the cell door nearest him, he yanks the thing open. "You're free."

Everest unlocks his door while Jade fumbles with the latch on hers. Tremont approaches the small man with various horns protruding from the top of his skull that Wes had broken out.

"Your wrists, I can get those off."

With a hesitant but curious stare, the man squeezes out of the opening and holds his arms out to Tremont. He anxiously looks at the lot of us. "Wh-what's happening?"

A large woman with dull blue skin and a long trunk for a nose steps around Everest and hugs the man covered in feathers Jade had freed. "Are you okay?" She squeezes him tightly with tears in her eyes.

"We're getting out of here, that's what," I tell them. "You can stick with us or flee at the first opportunity, but you'll be stuck in their territory unless you can find a hunter to let you out."

The fact that I'm still considered one turns my stomach. I don't want to be associated with these people—even if it is only by blood.

"What can we do to help?" The woman steps toward me. "I'm Pippa, this is Lo."

The quiet other prisoner joins us. "I'm Landry." He

rubs at his wrists, the same reaction everyone else has after finally getting those things off.

Not only are they uncomfortable, but they restrict our power by some kind of current it pushes into our body. The second we're no longer restrained by them, it's like that energy comes rushing back through us.

Mine has been on the fritz ever since I stepped foot in this place. Typically, I have certain abilities that come naturally, but whatever they did to me, it's rattled my core. I feel unsettled and foreign in my own skin. But given everything that's changed lately, I'm not at all surprised.

"We're escaping through twelve," I tell the newest members of our group. "And we're freeing every demon we can between here and there. Whatever you can do, whether it be fight alongside us, or help us explain to the prisoners what's going on. Just stay out of the line of fire and don't get killed."

Something I never thought I'd hear come out of my mouth—telling a demon *not* to die. The old me would be salivating at the thought of all these souls for the taking. That version of me is dead.

"We good?" I ask the group while realizing I've sort of put myself in charge here.

Wes steps to my side and presses his hand against my shoulder. "Ready when you are."

I draw in a long breath, giving myself a quick moment of reprieve in anticipation of what's waiting for us in the next sector. "Let's go." I motion for everyone to follow and take off into a sprint around the corner and down the corridor. With Wes at my side, I ask him, "Can you throw your fire?"

He nods and as if reading my mind, he increases his speed to get in front of me.

Like he's turning up the dial, his body flickers to life and flames dance over his skin, somehow not burning his clothes off. I stopped trying to understand the specifics of magic a long time ago. Still barefoot from his shift into hound form earlier, each step he takes leaves a soft trail of fire in his wake. It's kind of magnificent, really.

Wes plants his arms to his side, his fingertips pressed toward the floor. He ignites further, balls of fire forming in his palms. He throws the first one, causing chaos the second he rounds the corner into the next sector.

Men scream and cry out in pain, while others frantically try to regroup and attack the flaming man.

"Stay back unless you can fight!" I yell at my group.

I tally up the soldiers until I cannot keep track any longer and go to work eliminating them one by one. They duped us in the last sector by only having two guards. They tried to make us believe escaping would be easy in an attempt to get us to lower our inhibitions and fall victim to this ambush they planned. They massively underestimated how powerful we are both mentally and physically. I'm sure Parla thinks that her extensive torture and interrogation did a number on me, but that couldn't be further from the reality of this situation. All of their torture tactics fueled us to want to end each and every one of their lives *that* much more.

My only hope is that I'm the one who gets to drive a knife into her chest and watch the life leave her fucking eyes as she comprehends that I am the reason for her downfall.

Wes throws another ball of fire into the crowd, eliminating at least a half dozen guards. He glances over at me and goes back to snapping the neck of a man who approaches his side.

I kick a guy in the stomach and double him over, using the movement to slice his throat and turn my attention to another target.

Out of the corner of my eye, Everest punches a guard in the face and Tremont casts what appears to be a protective barrier around Jade so she can unlock a cell. I skim the bodies in an attempt to locate our other members in between jamming the sharp end of my blade into the people who stand between us and our freedom.

I spot Landry climbing up a pile of fallen men and then using his hands like suction cups, he slithers up the wall. He disappears through a crack in the ceiling that was probably formed by one of the various explosions lately. He may have abandoned us, but he's one less person I have to worry about keeping alive. He's made his own bed, and now he's on his own to figure out how to navigate this hell.

Kneeling to the ground, I spin in a circle and slice the knife through three different men's calves. They cry out and frantically search for the cause of their pain. I roll out of sight and thrust the knife into one of their chests.

Someone grabs a fistful of my hair from behind and yanks me off my center.

Always the fucking hair.

I reach up and latch onto the person's wrists to stifle their control over my body. Reeling my leg up, I throw the brunt of my force backward and slam my foot straight into their chest. The man heaves and loosens his grip enough that I can maneuver myself to face him. With his fingers desperately trying to cling to my head, I reach into my waistband to pull out a small knife and slice it against his forearm. I dig the blade deep, causing damage that he will bleed out from within minutes. He releases me completely and presses his other hand into the wound, stumbling and tripping over a lifeless body behind him.

"Fucking prick," I mutter once I'm free of him. I scan the floor for the first blade I had dropped when he attacked me, sighing when it's nowhere in sight.

A few bodies rush into me, knocking me down and pinning me under them. A flashback of that day I was lost under the scurni with Wes's power making me unable to speak trickles into my mind. I was furious with him for abusing his power that way, and when I was finally granted the ability to talk again, I gave him an earful for it. Hell, I may have even told him I hated him. In hindsight, I see the error in judgment he made, and realize he was only trying to keep me safe, despite using the absolute worst choice of words to do so. At that point, I still didn't know he had feelings for me, and he was doing everything he could to evade that part of him from rising to the surface. Maybe if we had embraced our connection sooner, we wouldn't be in this mess now.

I shove my palms into the concrete to gain some traction on my situation, wiggling my body to try to free myself of the dumbasses on top of me. My wrist gives out and launches a new steady ache throbbing down my forearm. I roll my eyes and let out a breath. I didn't make it this far to be smothered by some fucking guards.

"Wren!" a frantic voice calls out through the chaos.

"Under here!" I yell back, relieved at my ability to actually direct my savior to my whereabouts this time.

The load on my back lightens and the spots in my vision clear up with each body removed.

Once I'm uncovered, I use my non-injured hand to press up off the floor.

Wes helps me off the ground and tugs me to his body, squeezing me so tight I can barely fucking breathe.

"Wes," I mumble into him. "You're..."

He releases me, pressing his hands to my cheeks and scanning my face. "I thought I lost you."

"If I could stop almost being crushed to death, that would be great." I take a step but wince at the pain shooting up my leg. "Fuck," I blurt out, seeing the knife I was using earlier jammed into my thigh. "That's going to leave a bruise." I grip the handle and clench my jaw as I yank it free. Not allowing Wes to say a damn word, I glance up at him. "No, you cannot heal it, but you can use your flame to stop the bleeding."

A blast of light fills the space and a loud crashing sound follows. Whoever is bombing this place is getting dangerously close to where we are.

Wes shields me from the debris with his large body and uses his right hand to press his flaming finger against my exposed and bloody flesh. "You have to let me take care of you when we're done. I'm begging you."

I exhale deeply at having my skin melted together and pat his shoulder. "I'll think about it." I hobble over to a guard who has the upper hand on Everest and starting from the top of his back, I drag the knife in my grasp down to his waist. Immediately, he stops attacking Everest and screams out in agony. "You good?"

"Yeah, thanks." Everest pants and nods rapidly.

A demon with skin as black as night and a tail longer than its own body rushes past me, using said tail to penetrate a guard's throat and fling the man's frame off into the wall.

"Retreat!" One of the remaining guards calls out,

not waiting for anyone else to follow as he takes off down the corridor leading him to the next sector.

The newest member of our group swirls his tail around his legs and picks him up into the air before he can get away.

"I like him, who's that?" I ask Jade from her spot behind me.

"That's Rudy. Pretty polite guy if I may say so myself."

I chuckle. "Seems like it." I watch with a grin as the last of the guards scuttle up and attempt to get away.

Rudy sinks his claws into one of the guards and rips a long strip of flesh off his throat. He obnoxiously chews the meat and drops the body.

"Could use some table manners," I add.

I take in the sight of my team assembling around me, a few fresh members in tow, relief flooding in at everyone appearing decently unharmed. "Only lost one, that's good." I point to the spot in the ceiling where Landry had escaped out. "If anyone wants to follow suit, now's your chance."

A small woman with scales covering her cheeks and slits for a nose blinks a few times, her many eyelids showing with the movement. She mumbles something incomprehensible and climbs the wall. Her hands suction to the surface the same way that Landry's had.

"We're sticking with you," Pippa chimes in.

I skim the gazes of the rest of the group, noting the subtle nods of each member.

"Rudy," I call out down the corridor. "You lead the way."

We take off after him, no doubt exhausted and ready for this to all be over, but growing in numbers, our chances of making it out of here rising along with the morale.

Wasting no time, we clear the next three sectors without issue. Their guards have pulled back and are nowhere to be found. Do they not realize we're releasing their prisoners along the way, which is only strengthening our defenses against them?

I keep bracing myself around every corner, expecting them to advance on us, but it never happens. Have they truly given up and accepted the fact that they cannot win this war? If Parla has any say in it, she'd let every one of them die if it meant a chance at stopping us.

We clear the sector with the faded thirteen painted on the wall and pause before the last leg of our journey. There have only been small openings to escape along the way, either in the ceiling or in places too difficult to squeeze through. According to Everest, the biggest breach is sector twelve, giving us all the opportunity to escape. And if what he's saying is true, that's probably why the troops have been called back.

The likelihood of them rallying the brunt of their forces there is strong, meaning the worst of this battle is just around the next corner. But as I stand here, scanning the faces of these people, I'm struck with the realization that some things are worth fighting for—worth risking your life for. Their freedom is at the top of the list. They might have demonic blood running through their veins, but that doesn't make them any less deserving of their rights than anyone else in this realm. Parla claims that they are the evil of this world, and yet all I see are a group of terrified and tortured souls begging to be set free.

"Hey," Wes whispers while tucking a strand of my wild hair behind my ear. "In case I don't get the chance to say it..."

I shrug him off. "Nope, no goodbyes today, Romeo."

"That's not what I was going to tell you." He tugs me to his chest anyway. "I'm proud of you."

I hug him back briefly. "Be proud when we've made it out alive."

"Okay," he smiles down at me and presses his lips to my dirty forehead.

"You two make a cute couple." Jade nudges me with her elbow and then nods ahead of us. "They're going to try to ambush us, aren't they?"

I sense the nervous energy in the small space we're all crammed into. "Yes." I turn toward the crowd. "I want each of you to get out as soon as you can. Run for the forest and do not stop until you hit the barrier." I look to Everest. "You will go with them, get them out of here, you hear me?"

"What about you?" he asks me.

"I won't be far behind." I must see to it that every person in our group makes it to safety.

Pippa steps forward, a small group of demons gravitating toward her. "We'd like to continue on to the remaining sectors."

Tears well in my eyes but I blink them away. I've had a sinking feeling this entire time knowing we'd be leaving so many behind. I'd be lying if I said I wasn't conspiring to come up with some kind of plan to stay back and free them on my own, but with her help, and those volunteering to go with her, I can breathe a little easier. Still, I can't help but be consumed by the nagging selfishness of leaving them unprotected.

Rudy glides across the back of the crowd and takes his place with Pippa and her people. "I'll see this through." His voice is thick like tar.

"Thank you," I tell all of them.

Pippa steps toward me, enveloping me in her arms. "Bless you for not leaving us here." She gives me one final squeeze. "You are an angel."

If only she knew my past, if she could see the pile of bodies that would no doubt fill this very room and many more. She'd hate me. Hell, I hate myself enough for the both of us.

I focus on Everest. "You get them out, okay?"

He responds by inching closer to Jade, his body acting as a shield.

Collectively, our entire group moves down the final

corridor into the unknown. We don't run, we don't charge, we save our energy for the battle ahead.

When we approach the last leg, Wes leaves my side to lead us. My soul begs to be up there with him, but my brain knows it's the most logical formation. I will be with him soon enough. Either in death or free of this place. Both are an oddly comforting reality. This life has been torturous, and I'm not sure there's anything I can do to redeem the actions of my old self. I am ashamed of the person I was. Not even death can purge me from my sins, though.

Wes's entire body ignites into a beautiful flame seconds before he shoves through the door separating us from the other side.

I rush behind him, knives staged in both hands, readying to fight our way out of this place. A battle cry floats its way up my chest but falls flat when I blink around the vast and empty area. A chill creeps up my spine and an uncomfortable pit grows in my stomach. I swallow down the unease and watch the rest of the group funnel in.

My attention falls to the gaping crater on the side of the building. Rubble is littered on the floor of the room and piled haphazardly outside. Dust and fog fill the air but there's not a person in sight.

"This doesn't feel right," I mutter under my breath.

Are they waiting for us to escape? Is the trap actually outside these walls instead of in this confined room? What angle could Parla possibly be playing right now, and why have I not figured it out yet?

Wes tilts his hand upward and conjures a ball of fire in his hand. He glances over at me. "I hope this doesn't work." He throws the flaming thing into seemingly nothing, erupting the room into chaos.

Screams follow his attack and a few people who aren't immediately killed from the fireball flail their arms and frantically pat at them to extinguish themselves.

The barrier keeping the guards invisible flickers, showing some of them, then all of them.

My heart stutters at the sheer number of men standing around us, blocking our path to freedom.

I walked these people straight into a trap and now here we are, outnumbered and completely surrounded by people who wish nothing but to kill us.

15
WREN

I drive the knife in my right hand into a man's chest and yank it out quickly, moving on to my next target. Dodging a baton from a guard, I spin on my heel and crouch, shoving the sharp end of the blade into another guard's thigh.

His screams are a comfort to my soul—one less person standing in our way.

I'm kicked from behind and flipped around.

A man straddles my waist and pins me to the floor. "Remember me, you fucking bitch?"

The guard I had beat until his face swelled stares back at me. "Not really. You all look the same."

I wrap my legs around his torso and hold him tightly to my body, giving him little space to move.

His hot breath turns my stomach. "You think you can overpower me?"

"No," I tell him. I grip the collar of his standard

issued shirt and tug it down, latching onto it with my other hand and creating an X with my forearms. I pull tighter, dragging him to my chest and grinning at his surprise. "I know so." With nothing but the weight of our bodies and his shirt, I strangle him until his body stops convoluting in its attempts to get free.

I shove him off me and scan the ground for my knives. Panting from the effort of such an intimate kill, I locate one of the blades and turn back to my victim. Because one can never be too sure, I plunge the knife into his chest once, twice, three times. Blood splatters onto my face and only fuels my desire to bathe in it by the time this is all said and done.

A hand appears at my side and for a split second, my first instinct is to grab it and pull the person down with me. But when my gaze trails up to the demon it's attached to, I realize that it is not the enemy, but a fellow comrade.

I permit the man with horns protruding from his forehead to assist me off the floor. "Thank you."

Something I never thought I'd offer genuinely— thanks to a demon.

"Are you injured, ma'am?" He scans my face which is now splattered with crimson.

"No." At least not any more than I already was. My entire body aches and this battle will no doubt create more wounds that will need to be healed. That is, if I make it out alive. I've evaded death all my life, but what if this is when she finally welcomes me home.

The demon's eyes go wide as he focuses on something behind me. "Watch out." He shoves me aside and steps into the line of fire, taking a knife straight to the chest.

In a flash, I circle and plunge my blade into the attacker's neck, a fountain of red pouring from in its wake. I push him aside and catch the demon before he hits the floor. "Fuck." I cradle his head and scan the black ooze seeping from around the entry wound.

"P-p-pull it out." The demon remains still but manages to spit out those few words. "Please."

Gripping the handle, I comply and free him of the knife penetrating his chest. I press my hand into it to attempt to stop the flow.

"Wren." Wes's voice seems to float toward me.

I shift my head in his direction across the room. In complete and utter chaos, I was able to locate him with ease. I watch him snap a guard's neck and toss him aside.

He nods like he's accepting that I'm okay and goes back to work killing whoever is near him.

My attention flickers through the crowd, spotting anyone I can recognize. I search frantically for Jade, pausing when my sights land on Tremont, his hands outstretched and a steady flow of magic streaming out and blasting onto the opening to the outside world. A sheer barrier in place where there should be nothing. Tremont is trying to break it so our people can finally escape. Rudy stands guard near him, blocking any threat that comes his way. His tail wraps around a man and uses the body to knock down three others before violently slamming it into the concrete floor.

"I can heal," the demon in my arms mutters. "I just need a few minutes."

I blink down at him. "Really?"

"Can you buy me some time?"

"Of course." I look to my hand blocking the wound from sprouting. "What about this?"

"Place mine on it, if you will." His gaze darts down to his arm. "I'm afraid I'm a bit paralyzed." He lets out a sigh. "Distant cousin to the scurni."

I chuckle and do as he requests. "I'm familiar." I'll never forget being pinned under that fainting ogre.

What a terrible trait to inherit.

"I won't allow anyone to harm you." I gently set his head against the floor and rise to my feet. "I promise." Taking the knife that had been sunk into his chest, and that of the one I previously had, I renew myself to the war around us.

Pippa approaches, her footsteps thunderous and booming. "We held them off as best we could."

"Thank you." I note the demon barrier around me and my injured friend. "Help Rudy defend Tremont." I motion toward the only chance of us getting out of here. If he can't take it down, then we're trapped in this prison for good. Sure, we can kill every last one of them, but if magic is holding us in place, then we need a witch to break it.

The demons protecting me follow my order and rush through the crowd to maintain a stronghold with Rudy.

The guards feign confusion for a split second at their retreat but then quickly concentrate on their target.

"Come and fucking get me," I yell at them.

One by one they attack, their arms raised with their weapons poised and ready to strike.

Oh, how foolish of them to be so careless with their offense. Didn't their trainers teach them better? Clearly, we went to two entirely different facilities to learn our skills. Or maybe I'm just naturally not a fucking idiot like these guys are.

I grin, no doubt looking like a psycho with the dried remains of their friends caked on my face. Steadying my breath, I send the first knife flying through the air and landing it with deadly accuracy into the man's throat.

His arms lower and he clutches briefly at the thing wedged into his windpipe.

I watch carefully as the next man charges at me, biding my time, waiting for the perfect opportunity to strike. I seize it, ducking to block his blow and driving the weight of my entire body into my shoulder and knocking him to the floor. I reel my leg up and kick another man in his shin, buckling his leg in the wrong direction and disarming him. I turn and thrust each of my hands to the sides, one with a blade, the other outstretched and with nothing but brute force. I slide the blade out and quickly evade those two men as they fall into each other.

Another approaches, a bit more cautious than the rest. Is he the least stupid out of the bunch?

"Fucking traitor," he spits.

I'll take that as a no.

"What are you waiting for?" I ask him while sizing him up.

He's easily a foot taller than me, triple my weight. His muscles bulge the fabric of his shirt and instead of finding them intimidating, I'm repulsed. He's either the type of guy who eats nothing but protein and hits the gym three times a day or uses enhancements to cheat the system. The vein bulging from his forehead and the sweat accompanying it tells me that he's already exhausted where I'm only just getting started.

The guard unsheathes a sword from his side and extends it toward me.

"Is that supposed to scare me?" I laugh at him.

He nods to the dead man at my foot. "Go on, I'm waiting."

I glance down, catching the glint of the sword in my sights. "Step back," I tell him.

He raises his free hand into the air and complies while lowering his weapon.

Swiftly, I drag the heavy mass of the sword out from the corpse's control and familiarize myself with the weight of it in my hand. I tend to prefer smaller blades as they offer more agility, but if he wants to test my skills, I'll gladly oblige.

The guard strikes first in an attempt to catch me in a moment of weakness. I match his blow, the blades clanging loudly. My wrist aches at the impact but I push the pain aside. I don't have time to succumb to the discomfort now.

I counter, aiming for his neck and hoping for a quick win, but he anticipates my bluntness and blocks the attack. We go back and forth like this for what feels like an eternity, swinging and blocking, blocking and swinging.

He manages to nick me with the tip of the blade, cutting through the thickness of my armor top and slicing a thin layer of my flesh.

I grow furious at the defeat of him drawing first blood and match him by advancing quickly and grazing his brow.

He brings his hand up to the wound and looks at the blood that remains on his fingers. "You're going to pay for that."

"They say women are chatty, and here you are, refusing to shut up." I use his distraction to advance him again, but he counters my attack. I turn, skimming the crowd briefly to locate Wes, my reaction time stuttering when I don't spot him.

My breath catches as the blade slashes my thigh, and for a split second, I worry that this might be the end. I shake the thought and focus on the here and now. I refuse to let *this man* be my downfall.

I plant my feet firmly onto the floor and bend my knees. I swipe the sword through the air, landing it with a loud clang against his, and immediately strike him again, and again. I've been playing this to his pace, and if I want to end this, I have to change things up. I land another strike, turning myself completely around and hitting him from a different angle. This one finds a home against his calf, spurting blood as the blade slices through his flesh.

He cries out in agony and I advance, not wanting to waste another minute with this pathetic excuse of life.

I kick him off center and point the tip of my sword at his neck. "Checkmate."

His eyes widen and the alarm of actually losing settles into his features.

Sliding the sword down further, I position it near his heart. With a grunt, I thrust the long edge into his chest and savor the gasp of horror that escapes him. I leave him there to bleed out, staining the concrete like so many others before him.

"Wes," I cry out. I shove a guard and squint through the fight to find him. "Wes!" I yell. "Where are you?" My heart aches and uncertainty takes hold. I scan the bodies lining the floor and pray to any god that might be listening that Wes isn't among them.

Pippa holds her place next to Rudy, who is still

protecting Tremont as he maintains his magical connection to the wall holding us in.

Despite all of the dead around us, the number of guards doesn't seem to stop coming. It's like Parla has an endless supply of grunts at her disposal. And yet, she's nowhere to be fucking found.

If I could just kill her, maybe it would sever that idiotic and suicidal bond these guards share with her. Maybe then they would realize they cannot win this battle.

But, if it were the old me, I wouldn't have stopped until either everyone around me was dead or I had been killed. That knowledge is the one thing that assures me that death is the only option. There is no time to reason with them, not when they're determined to kill anyone that defies everything they believe in.

I gravitate toward the throng of guards that takes up one large section in the corner, fear unlike anything I've felt before boiling inside of me. What if Wes is in the center, beaten and bloodied to a point of no return? What if he's already gone? Wouldn't I know? Wouldn't I feel it? Or does our connection not work that way?

I grip onto the shirt of a guard and toss him aside, anxious to get to the core of their collective attention.

"Wes!" I shout into the space.

The guard I pushed latches onto me and drags me backward.

I elbow him in the face, crunching his nose under the force. "Don't fucking touch me." I kick him in the chest and he slams into the wall behind him with a thud.

His body slides down the hard surface and he remains motionless.

I turn to the crowd once more and watch as they take a step back.

Is this it? Are they finished? Have they inflicted all the damage they needed to?

I shake my head refusing to believe my worst fears.

Out from the center like a beacon in the night sky, Wes emerges, only he is no longer in his man form, but that of his hound. Towering over some of the men, he exposes his teeth and growls at them. In a flash, he pounces, ripping the head off one man's body and throwing it to the side. Another tries to evade him, but he latches onto his leg and drags him toward him. The man drags his fingers across the floor and screams as Wes sinks his claws across his shoulders and down his torso.

The hound's gaze meets mine and I'm met with those beautiful glowing red eyes.

I sigh and release the tension I didn't realize had built up within me.

My fated mate is alive, he's okay.

He lurches into the air but doesn't land his attack until the man has already hit me across the head.

I stumble and fall to my knees, hot liquid running down my forehead. My own blood trickles into my mouth and down the crook of my neck. My skull throbs and I struggle to blink through the stars appearing in my vision.

At least Wes is fine.

That alone is enough to keep the pain at bay.

A warm and furry head appears at my side and nudges my arm. He licks at my cheek and presses his cool nose to my face. The hound lets out a whimper.

"It's okay," I tell him while patting the top of his head. "I'm good." I rise to my feet, using Wes to help steady me.

It's then that I notice he's ripped apart at least a dozen guards in my momentary lapse.

"Good boy." I pat his head and stroke just under his ear.

He purrs and closes his eyes momentarily like he's enjoying the praise.

"We need to get out of here." I turn my attention to the rest of the room, noting how the majority of the guards are trying to penetrate the protection surrounding Tremont. We must be getting close to breaking it down if they're this determined to attack with that much force.

It must be a powerful barrier if he still hasn't broken through it yet, though.

With Wes at my side, I make my way over to the crowd, snatching a knife on the way and digging it into the back of a guard none the wiser. "Can you get me in there?" I ask Wes, watching as more soldiers flood into the room and approach our rear.

He dips his head and leans down, clenching onto a guard's ankle and dragging him from his position. He goes in for another and I use the opportunity to stab the next one.

"Pippa!" I call through the small opening. "I'm coming through."

"The hell you are," a guard blurts out when he spots me trying to get past him. He reaches for me but comes up empty-handed when Wes claims him with his inescapable grip.

I squeeze through, ducking and shoving men out of the way. At this point, it's like they're mindless robots doing whatever they can to disrupt us from continuing on our path to freedom. Their disregard for their own survival is sickening.

Pippa latches onto my forearm and tugs me the rest of the way through.

Rudy holds the line and allows us a chance to catch our breath.

"What's taking so long?" I ask her and nod to Tremont.

Pippa returns to her spot defending the attacks from the guards.

"I need more power!" he yells from his spot not too much further from me.

I step forward, doing everything I can to show a strong front despite feeling like my legs and body might actually give out from underneath me. "Take mine." I extend an arm. I might not have much to give, but I'd sacrifice every last drop if it meant getting these people their freedom.

Tremont side-eyes me and sighs. "You look worse for wear, Wren."

"This is no time for debate, sir. Whatever it takes. What do you need me to do?" I bring myself closer to him and ignore the new round of guards that have entered the confines of this room.

"It could kill you," Tremont warns.

"I don't fucking care, just tell me what to do." I grow frustrated with his lack of urgency.

"Place your hand in mine; I'll do the rest."

Without allowing him any more time to waste, I press my palm into his and mentally let down my defenses. I have no idea how this kind of transfer works, but I assume I cannot show resistance.

Tremont's entire body shakes and something electrical sparks to life between us. His stare widens, as if he's afraid of the connection that has us tethered.

I worry that it's not enough—that my power has dwindled too much and that I will not be of any help. I should have sent Wes through and had Tremont channel his power. But if this process means any chance of harm, I was the right person for it all along. I can deal with sacrificing myself, not anyone else.

"Is something wrong?" I ask him over the buzzing in my ears.

"I..." Tremont twists his free hand and a burst of white light floods out of it and pours into the barrier, shattering it with ease. He remains gripping my hand as he pulls me forward. "We must go, now."

I try to yank myself free but it's no use. I'm too weak and his hold on me is too strong. I crane my neck to peer behind me. "Everybody, run!"

Like a stampede of children on the last day of school, the demons who had been battling for their freedom turn and bolt out the opening. Wind rushes past my cheeks with each of them that escapes. I breathe in the air, noting the remnants of the explosions coating my lungs. I'll be grateful once we're away from here and can smell the freshness of the forest and appreciate the stillness of safety. Although, I'm not entirely sure that will ever come knowing what I know now.

Parla won't rest until she's brought me back here to use however she pleases.

If I stand any chance of defeating her for good, I have to get as far away from here as possible and regain my strength.

We all do.

Today's battle might be close to a win, but this war has only just started.

16
WREN

"Let go of me," I demand.

"I have to get you out of here; I promised." Tremont continues to pull me over the rubble, taking me further away from where I last saw Wes in hound form.

I wince from pain all over my body taking turns assaulting me. In my ankle, my thigh, my chest, my wrist—everywhere hurts. Every single inch of my frame aches from the never-ending torment it's endured. Will the agony ever end?

"I will fucking kill you if you don't release me. Mark my words, I am not someone you want to cross."

At this, Tremont drops my hand. He turns to face me, his serious gaze meeting mine. "Wes has shifted, am I correct?"

I nod silently.

"Nothing will stop him from finding you. But if you do not get out of here, you're putting him in danger. You're putting everyone in danger."

I grit my teeth and roll my eyes. How dare this complete stranger be so damn correct?

Jade reaches my side, Everest in tow. "Are you okay?" Her gaze trails down my face and over my battle-worn body.

"I'm fine. Are you?"

"Yes, but we need to go." She goes to take a step, but I reach out and stop her.

"Have you seen Wes?" A piece of my heart breaks in anticipation of her answer.

"No, I'm sorry. He's Wes though, are you seriously worried?" She laughs it off like we didn't just escape from the worst possible place in all of Prania.

"You aren't?"

"There she is," a man calls out from the side of the building.

Tremont grips my elbow. "Come. Now."

I yank away from him but follow the lot of them, not because I want to, but because it's true. I'm the key to Parla's master fucking plan and in my weakened state, I'm too vulnerable to hang around and allow myself to be captured again.

We climb over the fallen remains caused by the explosions and take turns shimmying along the small gap between the debris. Everest leads the way and stops for us at every spot, making sure all four of us are through before continuing. My chest aches at the distance growing between me and Wes, but I know I cannot go back for him, that I must carry on.

A small group of demons rip a few guards to shreds as they try to subdue them. The demons hungrily look for their next target once they've completed that mission, not lingering their sights on us for long, knowing that we are not a threat.

"We're going to have to run past that tower." Everest points to the thing in the close distance. He lowers his finger to the tree line off further. "If we can make it there, we should be able to disappear."

I beg my soul to contact my mate and tell him to hurry the fuck up. He'll be trapped in this territory if he doesn't make it in time. And regardless of what he or anyone else has in mind, I refuse to leave this place without him.

"See that break in the wall?" Everest steadies his hand at the thing just past the guard tower. "That's where we'll cross."

I size up the distance between here and there and do a mental assessment of my injuries. Between those and the bit of power I lent Tremont, I'm running on fucking fumes at this point. I've been beaten and torn down, but this is almost an all-time low.

Nothing really compares to when Wes saved me from dying alone in that building.

And here I am, leaving him to the same fate.

The only difference is that he's in much better shape to fend for himself than I was back then.

"Are we ready?" Everest spares a glance at all of us. "Let's go."

We start off side by side, but fall into a formation of two by two, my weak form trailing to the rear with each step we take.

Tremont slows his pace to join me.

"Go ahead," I tell him while shifting my focus to the tower growing larger as we get closer.

Shouldn't they be stopping us? Shouldn't *something* be preventing us from escaping? Or are things really that bad that they no longer have a hold on who comes and goes from here?

Everest quickly scales the opening in the wall, pulling himself up and over the edge, and disappearing onto the other side. Jade follows suit, looking back briefly before she is no longer visible either. Tremont and I catch up to the structure.

"Go on." I look to the tower and then at the prison we just came from.

People scatter here and there, and from this distance, I can't tell if the demons remain the ones in control. Still, there is no sign of Wes, and that alone threatens to break me completely.

"Go on, damn it," I urge him again. "I'm right behind you."

Tremont latches onto my shoulder. "He made me promise that I'd get you out. Don't make me break that."

I shake him off me. "No one is breaking any promises." Although, I can't be entirely sure, because if Wes doesn't show up soon, I don't think I'll be able to withstand the visceral urge to go back for him.

Tremont climbs up and hops down onto the other side, leaving me here alone.

I hesitate, my hand positioned to follow him, my heart begging me to go the other way.

"Come on, Wes," I whisper. "Where are you?"

And like a gift from the fucking universe herself, I catch a flash of his black fur while he's running after a guard. He tackles the man to the ground and claws at his chest before dismounting him and moving on to another target.

He's not here with me, but he's safe, he's alive, and that's all that matters for now.

I tighten my hold on the wall and hike my leg up to the fractured part of it.

Looking back one last time, I'm thrown through the opening when the base of the tower to my right explodes, sending fragments flying and shattering against the stone surface. Some manage to make it through with me, little spikes of concrete impaling into the back of my legs. I gasp and clutch my chest while doing a quick scan of my body to make sure the damage is only minimal. I raise my head and count the bodies huddled together and then spot two others off in the distance. Something oddly familiar about the shape of them.

"Wren," Tremont calls out.

Ignoring him, I stand, my feet having a mind of their own, walking toward the other people. As their forms go from a blur to something more defined, my pace picks up until I'm sprinting in pain, each step a reminder of how damaged I really am.

I press the mark on my neck and blink through the tears that fill my eyes.

Like he's sensing my presence, his large figure turns in my direction, his mouth falling open at the sight of me.

Bo drops the device clung in his hand and slaps Dash on the shoulder before taking off.

Emotions spill over at seeing them, both of them, alive and well.

I've felt the connection to Bo this entire time, with moments of him getting further away and then approaching again, but he was always there. Even with Dash's phoenix nature, I still worried that something might change about his powers, and without having that same connection to him, could never grow comfortable with the uncertainty of the situation.

Bo takes the final step in front of me and lifts me into his arms, pulling me from the ground and spinning me in a circle. "Oh, Birdie."

I wrap myself around his neck and breathe in his musky scent, allowing my shape to melt into his and savoring the comfort he brings. How fucking strange that we started out absolutely hating each other and now I'm at home in his embrace.

He gently lowers me onto the ground and holds me at an arm's length. "You look like shit."

I laugh and punch his shoulder, wincing at the pain it causes my wrist. "It's good to see you, too."

Dash finally approaches, his strides much shorter than Bo's.

I sigh and take in the sight of his beautiful features while I come to terms with the fact that he's real. That he's actually standing in front of me.

He pauses and does the same, his eyes glistening.

Extending my arms, I cautiously limp over to him, no longer able to hide behind my ruse.

Carefully, he pulls me into him and hugs me. He drags in a long breath and kisses the top of my head. "We were so worried."

"You're not the only one." I rest my head against his chest and listen to the thumping of his heartbeat. A melody I could hear on repeat and never grow tired of, a steady reminder that he is still alive.

"What, no hug for me?" Jade calls out from behind me.

Bo's mouth drops open further than it did when he spotted me, and he stands there like he's stuck in place. "No fucking way."

Jade runs over to him and wraps her arms around his broad chest. "Missed you, asshole."

Bo softens his resolve and squeezes her. "I can't fucking believe it." He steadies his gaze on the other two members of our group. "Who are they? Where's Wes?"

"About that..." I rub at my neck, unsure of where to start.

"He's fucking *dead*?" Bo growls and releases Jade, shoving her behind him and squaring off to Tremont and Everest.

I step between them. "No, you irrational fool. He's just...occupied." I point to the guys. "This is Everest, he's..." I glance at Jade but decide to keep my mouth shut about that one. Another secret that isn't mine to tell. "He's been kind to us, and I expect you to show him the same respect." I point to Tremont. "This is Tremont, he broke the barrier keeping us locked in there."

Bo shakes hands with both. "A hunter and a witch, interesting." He narrows his gaze at them and then at me. "I don't trust them."

I smack his shoulder. "You didn't trust me either, and look where that got us." I place my hand on Dash's back. "This is Dash. Dash, Tremont and Everest."

Dash nods his head politely and leans into my touch.

Jade takes us in, noting the closeness and comfort we bring each other. "Are you two a thing, too?" She raises her brow at me and Dash.

"We're...not *not* a thing."

"Interesting." Jade doesn't add anything else.

Everest reverts to the current, more pressing, situation. "We need to get under cover." He motions to the tree line in the near distance. "That should do."

I wave at Bo to get his attention and lower my voice. "What was that thing in your hand back there?"

Bo blinks a few times like he's trying to recall a memory. "Detonator," he grins.

I smile, too. "That was you two blowing shit up?"

Dash wraps his arm around my shoulder. "Had to get you and Wes out of there somehow."

Speaking of, it would be fucking great if he would hurry up and meet us already. The relief of seeing him still alive was only temporary and it becomes more fleeting with each moment that passes.

Everest leads us away from the prison encampment and toward the forest surrounding the place. My heart stays put, begging with my feet to stop moving and go back for Wes. It's not right to leave him. I guess now that his hound has returned, he's not exactly alone. But that arrogant little shit has led me astray before, what if he does the same to Wes?

Bo places his large hand on the small of my back and glances down at me while Dash stays at my other side and the rest walk ahead. "Don't do that to me ever again." His stare is so intense a chill floats up my spine. "You could have died."

"I thought you wanted me dead." I swallow the lump that forms in my throat.

"Not anymore, Birdie."

He moves his hand up to the side of my face where he tucks my hair behind my ear.

It's strange to see him this...soft.

Bo is cruel, callous, and arrogant as hell. Our time apart must have really done a number on him if it's cracked that hard exterior.

His demeanor shifts from worry to curiosity. "Was there a woman...an older woman, with Wes?"

"Um, no. Why? Should there have been?"

Bo raises a brow at me. "Not with Jade?"

It's then that I realize who he's referring to, despite not having any clue who the person was. "No. I overheard Jade tell him they didn't make it." I glance at Jade walking ahead, her body gravitating toward Everest. Does Bo notice that the two of them like each other?

His jaw tenses and he nods stiffly.

"Who was it?" I ask him.

Bo sighs and rubs at his neck. "Essentially...Wes's mother."

I stop dead in my tracks, dropping Dash's hand. "We can't just leave him."

The group turns toward me and Tremont is the first to speak.

"I promised him I'd get you to safety. We aren't quite there yet."

"This *safety* you speak of," I quip. "Doesn't exist. Not in here, not out there, it's a hopeless cause."

"Birdie." Bo steps toward me with a gentle approach, his voice low. "The weird man is right."

"I'm standing right here, you know." Tremont folds his arms over his chest. "I'm only trying to help."

"I don't care," Bo tells him without turning around. He keeps his eyes on me. "We have to go; Wes will join us when he's done."

A group of demons hop the wall where we had come from not too long ago and runs toward us.

Bo exposes his teeth, and a low growl escapes him. He steps in front of me and points his arm to the ground, his razor-sharp talons appearing on the tips of his fingers.

I manage to wiggle past his defenses. "They're no threat to us," I tell him.

The herd of creatures jogs in our direction and slow their pace when they approach, each of their eyes going wide when they spot Bo. They crane their necks to look up at him but then quickly avert direct eye contact.

"Sorry, sir. Permission to speak, sir?"

Bo narrows his gaze at them and I elbow him.

"Yes," he spits out.

"It's with great urgency that you must go. They're vacating the premises, sir."

"And what's so terrible about that?"

The rest of our group steps a little closer to get in better range of the conversation at hand.

"I overheard the guards speaking that they're going to unleash a toxic poison on any remaining person left within the vicinity. Since we cannot escape the territory on our own, it's their way of ensuring we never do." The young demon's voice shakes with each word spoken.

I skim the faces of his friends, a look of terror on all of them.

Another round of demons crosses over the border and runs toward the tree line we're headed to. They divert their route and head over to us, stopping behind the first group like they're here for guidance.

Soon, there are nearly thirty creatures of various shapes and sizes looking to Bo for help.

"You don't need me," I turn to my people. "Everest can get you out. I can go back for Wes."

"In that condition?" Bo runs his hand through his dark hair and grunts. "Damn it, Wes." He glances to the place we just escaped. "I'll retrieve the little shit." He stares directly into the crowd of demons. "Go with them, they will set you free."

A collective murmur sounds from the demons.

"You won't be able to find him," I blurt out.

Bo has never seen Wes in his hound form, at least to my knowledge. I'm pretty sure Wes shifted for the first time in the prison after we marked one another.

"What aren't you telling me?" Bo stares down at me.

"I..."

Tremont clears his throat, bringing Bo's attention

from me to him. "Wes would want you all to get out while you can. He wouldn't wish for any of you to attempt to retrieve him."

Bo widens his shoulders. "And what do you know about what he wants?"

Tremont stands his ground. "I know that he cares about her very much."

Everest joins Tremont at his side. "I've seen first-hand what Wes is capable of, and I have no doubt that he can take care of himself. You'd be putting yourself at risk if you leave. And these people…" He motions to the crowd growing around us. "Need you."

Dash steps forward. "I'll go."

"No," at least a few of us say at the same time.

Dash lowers his head and returns to where he was previously standing.

I extend my arm and latch onto his hand. "No offense."

Tremont twirls his wrist and throws a burst of magic in between us and the wall we climbed over. "There, none of you will go back."

"What the hell did you just do?" I release Dash once again and yell at Tremont.

"It's for your own good, for everyone's own good. Now, we need to go."

A flashing light goes off in the distance, and an eruption of something shimmering rains down on the area it had exploded over.

"It's begun, sir," the demon speaking for the rest tells Bo.

Bo presses his eyes shut and rubs his temple. When he opens them, it's like a final decision has been made. He bends at the waist and swoops his arm around my legs, hoisting me into the air and over his shoulder. "Sorry, Birdie."

I pound on his back and try to wiggle my way free. "Let me down, you big buffoon." I continue hitting him until my face tingles from being upside down.

"It's better this way," Jade adds once I stop demanding to be released.

"If something happens to Wes," I mumble. "I will kill every single one of you." Except maybe Dash—he didn't exactly do anything wrong here. And it's not as though he could overpower Bo. I can't blame him for something he has no control over.

I lift the hem of Bo's shirt and press the soft skin on his lower back between my fingers.

Bo grips my thigh and maintains a hold on me with one arm. "Stop pinching me, Birdie."

"I will if you let me down." My body aches from the position he has me in, each step is a jab to every bit of pain I was already experiencing.

"Not until we're on the other side of the barrier."

"You're hurting me," I tell him, painting the guilt on thickly.

In a flash, he maneuvers me from over his shoulder

and into his arms. He cradles me to his chest and continues walking without faltering. "Better?"

I poke the side of his face. "I can walk, you know."

He glances down at me. "I didn't. But that's great, you should be really proud of yourself."

I prod at his cheek again. "Bo...this is fucked up."

This time he doesn't look at me when he speaks. "What's fucked up is you putting yourself in danger over and over again for no fucking reason."

"You really care that little of Wes that you'd leave him behind?"

"I care enough that I'm letting him do what he needs to do."

"What's that supposed to mean?"

Bo sighs. "Think about it, Birdie. Wes lost his mother. What do you think he's doing?"

Killing any and every one that could have possibly had something to do with it.

I cross my arms over my chest but don't respond. I don't dare tell Bo that he might be right.

When I saw Wes for that split second, his hound was ripping guards apart.

Is it possible that Wes could sense that I was in good hands and that's why he chose to separate himself from me to go on his murder spree? Am I the only one who is suffering from the distance between us? Like there's a hole forming in my chest and can only be remedied by my fated mate. There were once two gaping pits formed from being torn from Dash and Bo, but now those have been patched, and another has opened in Wes's absence.

What if we're never reunited? What if Wes is taken down by the poison and is never seen again? What if I could have saved him but Bo wouldn't let me? Would I ever be capable of forgiving him if I lose Wes forever?

I wipe a tear that rolls down my cheek.

"I'm sorry, Birdie."

17
WREN

The cluster of freckles on the side of Bo's face begins to blur the more I stare at it. It's bittersweet to be in his arms. Partly because I'm exhausted and the comfort he brings is a welcomed change to the recent chaos, but given the circumstances, I'd rather it not be so he could hold me captive from going back for Wes.

My entire body aches, inside and out. From old wounds and new, and from internal scars that won't seem to mend. Yet, they're ripped open, the freshness of them feeling like they happened just yesterday.

The silence of this journey into the woods has left me alone with my thoughts and angry at Bo. I'm aware I shouldn't be, but it's difficult when he's the one quite literally stopping me. Wes would want it this way, hell, he made Tremont promise it into action. None of this makes it any easier to stomach that Wes is out there, alone, dealing with his own physical and mental struggles.

I've never been the type to sacrifice myself for another, yet somehow, it's all my soul drives me to do. Perhaps I'm overcompensating for the lifetime of torment I've plagued this world with. A little voice in my head tells me no amount of selflessness will ever be enough to erase what I've done.

But that won't stop me from trying.

It's hard to believe that I was the real monster after all.

"Up ahead." Tremont motions through the dense forest. "Can you hear the buzzing?"

Bo clenches his jaw before looking down at me through his thick lashes. "Birdie." He tries a gentle approach, but it comes out rough. He clears his throat and speaks again. "Think I can set you down now or are you going to make a run for it?"

"Are you going to let me go if I do?" I ask him while considering my options.

"No."

I exhale dramatically. "Fine."

"Fine, what?"

"I won't run." Because the efforts would be wasted and only continue to add to the drama and danger, and we all need a lot less of that around here. Bo's strides easily triple the length of mine, along with his supernatural speed and the fact that he's not beaten and bruised. I wouldn't make it out of his arm's reach without him catching me.

"Good girl," he tells me.

"That doesn't mean I won't be thinking about it though."

Bo gently sets me onto the ground but remains firmly in place like he's assessing whether I'll actually take off or not.

I step forward to our small, original group, my footing wobbly at the pain shooting up my leg.

Dash reaches out and steadies me, his warm touch a comfort to my soul.

Damn did I miss this red-headed man. What I wouldn't give for uninterrupted time with both Dash and Bo, just to stare at their faces and hug them over and over. I'd be lying if I said I hadn't been worried I would never see either one of them again. Up until today, the rumors of Rock Bridge had proven true. No one had ever made it out of there alive. And now, here we all are, a testament that sometimes, things change. I shouldn't assume either of them would want the same though, just like I shouldn't have marked Wes without his consent. A moment that will continue to haunt me.

Something deep within me told me to act, to latch onto his neck the same way he had done mine. I needed to taste his blood on my tongue, to feel his flesh break under the weight of my bite. I'd never had those urges in my entire life, and in the moment, they completely consumed me. It wasn't until I saw the shock and terror on his face that I realized I made a mistake, that I had disgusted him with such a repulsive act.

Whether it was him marking me, or a combination of the both of us, it brought his hound side fully to the surface, and at the very least, I am grateful for that.

I recall Wes, in the moments after shifting into his man form, reaching out to me. He held my hand and pulled me to him. Would he have done that if he didn't want me anymore?

"Wren." Everest snaps his fingers in front of my face. "You in there?"

I blink and nod. "Yeah, sorry. What's up?"

"As you know," he says. "The barrier will only take one through at a time. Since we both hold the key to granting access, we should work in tandem."

"Of course, yeah." I reach out and waft my hand through the air to feel the forcefield in question. The electricity of it tickles my fingertips like a sort of *hello*.

"We should get started." A burst sounds off in the distance, another dose of poison being spread across the confines of the prison. It's only a matter of time until we're dosed, too, killing whatever remaining creatures are trapped within the barrier. I squint my eyes to see where we just came from, not a single black tuft of fur in sight. My soul pleads with him to appear, to be okay.

Everest looks up to Bo. "Can you assemble them in two single-file lines?"

Bo laughs, almost like he's imagining order among a massive group of frantic demons.

One of them pushes through to the front, shoving whoever he can to make space. "What's fucking taking so long?" He's scared, but this is no way of getting things done.

The polite demon who spoke for the rest gets pushed down onto the ground.

Bo snatches the aggressor, snapping his neck and tossing him aside. "Would anyone else like to die today?" His voice carries over the now silent crowd. "No? Then make two fucking lines. And if one of you so much as sneezes on the person in front of you, I will personally rip the flesh from your skin and pluck your eyeballs from their sockets. Do you understand?"

A collective murmur fills the space as the demons agree with the terms of their arrangement.

Bo reaches to help the fallen demon up and swats some of the dirt caked to his side away.

"Th-thank you, sir."

Dash assists me closer to the barrier, holding me steady as I place my hand on its nearly invisible surface.

Everest approaches a few feet away and repeats the same movement. He calls out to the demons that are waiting impatiently patient, "One at a time from each line, please."

The first of both step through the border and turn back briefly. As if suddenly realizing they're finally free, they nod their heads and take off, their bodies disap-pearing within seconds.

"Next!" I yell into the crowd.

With each demon that passes through and the time that keeps seeming to tick by, my concern for Wes only grows. Three more blasts have gone off in the sky, only making the window of breathable air in this place smaller and smaller. What if he's trapped somewhere and needs help? What if the poison has already taken him from this world?

He promised he'd find me in our next life, but what if I'm still alive in this one? I trail my gaze to the beau-tiful man at my side, holding me from collapsing, and the arrogant alpha standing guard at the base of the assembly. How could I leave these two to be with Wes, but how could I ever be happy if I stayed? Both options tear my heart apart, and I'm not sure which is better—which is worse.

"He'll be here," Tremont leans in and whispers.

I glance over at him. "How can you be so sure?"

"A connection like that is impossible to sever."

I crane my head to assess how much longer the lines are, but the more demons that go through, the more that seem to appear. A fog creeps through the forest, alerting me that our time is running out.

Steadying my gaze on Everest, I nod toward the impending doom. He takes it in and motions for the next demon to step through.

"Jade, Tremont, we need to send you over." I do a poor job hiding the urgency in my voice.

"We aren't going without you," she tells me.

"You don't have a choice." I look to Dash. "That goes for you, too."

Dash shakes his head. "Not happening. I'm not leaving you behind again."

Tremont chimes in, "I made a promise."

"Fuck your promise," I blurt out.

Bo slides his shirt over his head and rips at the fabric. He approaches and shows me the section in his hand. "I'm going to secure this over your mouth and nose, okay?"

I tip my head toward the crowd much further in the danger zone than I am. "Help them first."

"No." Bo ties the thing around my head, covering my airway. He breaks off another section and gives it to Jade, then the rest to Dash, leaving himself empty-handed.

I breathe in his scent and it weirdly calms the chaos raging within. It's a temporary fix, but I welcome it all the same.

"Everybody, listen up." Bo walks over to the demons. "If you can, remove your shirt and fasten it over your face, or whatever you breathe through. Move the lines horizontally instead of vertically to get everyone out of the line of the fog. Do not panic, I repeat, do not panic. If I witness anyone forcing their way up the line, I will make your death much more painful than that of the poison." He scans the crowd. "Are there any sick, elderly, or children?"

A little girl steps out of the throng of people and stands in place, not daring to move any more than she already has.

Bo spots her and immediately stalks to her. He kneels in front of her, saying something I cannot make out from this far. The two exchange a few words and he extends his hands. She steps forward, allowing him to pick her up and hold her at his side.

She wraps her small arms around his neck and holds on tightly while he carries her over.

"You." Bo points to a woman with rainbow-colored hair a few people back in the line. "Come here." He sets the little girl gently on the ground near me and motions over to Everest. "You go through over there. Make sure she gets somewhere safe."

The woman nods without another word, complying with the order given by this alpha.

I pull a knife out of my waistband and hand it to the child. "Here." An offering that, no doubt, must look out of place, but in this world, might be the one thing that helps keep her alive.

"Thank you," she whispers before stepping across the barrier.

Bo turns back to the crowd, scanning for anyone else that might need to go through with more urgency than the rest.

"Next," I tell the demon waiting near me.

Tremont drags his already tattered shirt over his head and grips the fabric, ripping it apart. He hands it to Jade, who secures it around Everest's face, and uses the rest for himself.

"Can't you magic this away?" I ask him, unsure of the restraints of his skills. Can't he magic this all away? The barrier? The poison rain? The fucking administration of this place?

"I am no longer as powerful as I once was." His words seem to have an underlying meaning he isn't quite saying.

This isn't the time or place for me to question him, though. Perhaps if we make it through this, I will learn more about this mysterious man.

The line of demons finally starts to shorten, but the fog approaching is moving quicker than we can get through. A few on the end cough and choke and bury their faces further into their pathetic coverings.

If it's this bad for them, Wes must be trapped in it somewhere.

I urge them through the opening and look at my friends. "Jade, you need to go next. We're running out of time." I glance at the man holding me steady. "You, too, Dash."

Bo rushes over with a limp body in his grasp.

I can't make out who or what it is, but I know the person needs to get to fresh air soon if they're going to make it.

"Can you stand?" Bo positions the person upright

near Everest, steadying them with a gentleness that is so unlike his natural behavior. He cranes his neck over to my side and focuses on the man about to step through. "Get her after you go over."

The man hurries across and rushes over to grab onto her hand. The two stay with each other until both of them are out of sight, no longer a concern of ours.

Ten demons on each side turn into nine, then eight.

The thick fog creeps further in, the remaining demons holding their breath and plugging their airways.

It's not until the last of them are through that Jade and Tremont enter the line.

Tremont stares directly at me. "You better be right behind me or I'm coming back for you."

"Dash, Bo." I urge the two of them to go through, leaving only me and Everest in the danger zone. I cough as the poison teases my lungs with its deadliness.

"We aren't going through until you do." Bo stands firmly in place, his jaw tight and his body rigid.

I swallow and shift my focus to him, to Dash, to Everest. If Dash and Bo don't go through, that means Everest can't either, because there's no way he's going to cross without granting them access first. My gaze skims the forest beyond, my eyes stinging from whatever they unleashed in the sky.

No Wes in sight.

How can I put three other lives in danger because of

one person? One person who happens to be my fated mate. How can I prioritize his life over theirs, over my own? Especially when every single part of me is screaming to find him, to save him, and at worst, die with him.

"Mother fucker," I blurt out, furiously stepping through the barrier. I suck in a fresh breath of air and blink through the tears I can no longer control.

Jade holds onto my shoulders, rubbing them with what I assume she thinks is a comforting touch.

Dash joins us a moment later, his own lifeforce desperate for the freshness this side brings.

The fog grows thicker and I can barely make out the shape of Bo until he's crossed over. Despite his head-strong persona, I can tell how relieved he is once he's joined us.

I step closer, squinting to find Everest through the all-consuming haze.

Jade drops her hands from my shoulders and moves toward the wall of white that has formed. "Where is he? Why hasn't he come yet?"

Her worry for Everest is something similar to what I've felt this whole time for Wes, only she's just now understanding what I've been experiencing.

If I weren't freaking out myself, I'd probably say something snarky about her finally grasping what I've been saying all along.

But with each passing second, I become more concerned with not just Wes, but Everest, too. The goal was for us all to make it out of here alive, not lose some of us in the final hours.

My heart pounds harder, my stomach turning at the possibility that Jade and I might both lose someone we love today.

"I'm going back." Bo steps forward but I reach out and grab onto his arm.

"The hell you are." I place myself in front of him. "If he's dead you'll be trapped." Before any of them can stop me, I burst through the barrier and onto the other side.

"Wren, is that you?" Everest stands with his hand still firmly pushed against the wall.

"What the fuck are you doing?" I yell at him.

He coughs and holds the shirt tightly on his face. "I saw something."

A flicker of hope sparks inside of me. Could it be true? Or is Everest going crazy from the poison flowing within him?

"You need to save yourself." I tilt my head toward freedom. "Hold them off, please."

"You know I can't do that," he barely chokes out.

I use his moment of weakness to approach him, and with the little bit of strength I can muster, I shove him to the other side.

I turn my attention back to the blinding fog and pray for a miracle or a swift death. My throat tightens and I know I should follow him, but I refuse to accept anything other than those two options.

18

DASH

I've only just gotten her back and she's gone again.

I expect to see her face cross over, but instead, it's that of Everest, the guy who is fixated on Jade.

Bo snatches him by the collar of his plain white T-shirt and lifts him off the ground. "What the fuck did you do?"

"I...I saw something."

"What do you mean *you saw something*?" Bo spits out through his gritted teeth.

"Let go of him," Jade cries out, scratching at Bo's arm. "You're hurting him."

"He's going to wish he was fucking dead when I get through with him if she doesn't..."

"A flash of red," Everest interrupts. "I thought—I thought it was Wes."

Tremont presses his hand to the wall of white and

243

closes his eyes. A second later, he opens his mouth. "She's alive. I can sense her."

Bo drops Everest onto the ground with a thud. "I'm going in."

I step in front of him. "If anyone's going after her, it's me. If I die, it doesn't matter."

"The hell it does," Jade blurts out from her spot next to Everest.

"No." I shake my head. "You don't understand... I'm..." I pause, unsure if I should actually say it out loud. Is it supposed to be a secret? Will it put these people in danger if they know? Aren't we all in as much peril as we possibly can be? I find the words slipping out anyway. "A phoenix."

Jade stares at me like I grew a horn out of the center of my forehead. "What?"

"So, if I die, I'll come back. No big deal."

Bo steps around me. "You don't know if there's an expiration on that Dash. You can't just volunteer to die whenever the opportunity presents itself."

"Oh, and you can?" I shove his solid chest. "What are the chances you resurrect, huh? Zero. At least with me, there's hope."

"No one is dying, today." Tremont keeps his palm against the wall. "There's a secondary presence."

"That's it." Bo takes off toward the barrier. "They could have sent someone to finish her off."

Tremont uses his free hand to throw a blast of

magic at Bo, holding him firmly in place. "I could do without the threats that are no doubt coming."

Bo starts to mouth off but stops at being called out for it. His pleading gaze locks onto mine.

"Don't make me restrain you, too, Dash." Tremont closes his eyes and tilts his head back toward the wall. Slowly, he steps away, but keeps his blasting energy pointed at Bo to keep him from going after Wren.

A flash of white, not dull and drab like the fog consuming the other side, but bright and comforting, momentarily explodes before us. Flames replace the light and once I'm able to blink through the chaos, a large shape appears.

Giant and standing on all fours with onyx fur and sharp, exposed fangs, rises from the burst of color. The fog that made it through dissipates, and a small body remains on the ground.

I rush over, skidding to a stop beside her.

The massive hound growls at me but I go to her anyway.

"Wren," I mutter while positioning her head off the ground and into my lap.

"If you don't let me go," Bo wrangles with the force-field Tremont is using to hold him in place. "I have to get her away from that..."

The creature rubs at Wren's ankle with his snout and then peers up at me.

My mouth falls open. The creature is no stranger at

all. Those eyes staring back at me belong to none other than…

"Wes?" Jade clutches her chest as she takes in the sight of him.

"No fucking way," Bo adds. He shrugs off the last of Tremont's magic and runs over to Wren's other side.

She opens her beautiful eyes and brings her hand up to her face, tugging down the fabric and drawing in a deep breath. "I see the dogs out of the bag." Wren pats the fur on the top of Wes's head. "Help me up." She extends her hand toward me and uses the other to press off the ground and rise to her feet. "Took you fucking long enough," she tells Wes.

He whimpers and nudges his head against her leg again.

"I'm sure we're all stunned by the recent events, but we should put as much distance as we can between us and this place." Wren flits her attention at the fog blasting the barrier around the prison.

Everest rises to his feet and runs his hand through his hair. "I have a place not too far from here. We can regroup and go from there."

"Is it warded?" Wren asks him.

He nods.

～

We make it to Everest's safehouse within an hour, just in time for the protective barrier Tremont projected around us to wear off once we stepped inside.

Tremont stumbles and catches himself on the wall. "That took a lot out of me, I apologize."

Bo sets Wren down on the floor, only now allowing her out of his grasp, like he's been afraid she might disappear on him this whole time.

I can't be certain, but I wouldn't be surprised if there's a fated bond there, too. In all my time in this realm with Bo, I've never witnessed him so...captivated by another. Stale bread and killing—yes. But a person, definitely not.

"Nice place," I tell Everest while I scan the vast modernness of this home. It's nothing like the shanty the guys and I rest our heads at, and it's even a step up from what Wren had shown us.

"Thanks." Everest nervously rubs his neck. "It was my brother's."

The past tense word choice doesn't evade me.

"And he's where?" Bo chimes in.

"Dead." Everest steps further into the front area and points down a long hallway. "There are bedrooms down the hall, bathrooms in both. The water should be hot, and if you check the closets, there should be spare clothes." He pauses on Wren and Jade. "Although they may be a little big for the both of you."

"I'm fine with this," Wren skims her hand along the side of her body.

"I'm going to get cleaned up. I suggest you all do the same." Everest stalks back over to the door and turns the lock to the fastened position. "I'll put food on once I'm finished."

Tremont offers his thanks and follows the path Everest had instructed, disappearing into the room on the left.

"Come on," Wren says as she limps in the direction Tremont had gone. "You said there's another bedroom?" She glances over her shoulder at Everest.

"Last one on the right."

Bo locks his sights on Jade when she gravitates toward Everest. "Where the fuck do you think you're going?"

"I'm not a child anymore, Bocephus." Jade keeps her arms folded over her chest, unmoving to her brother's dominance.

Wren sighs and backtracks, latching onto Bo's hand and dragging him away from his sister. "I said come on." She meets my gaze and tilts her head, insinuating that I should follow, too. "Wes, Dash."

Wes swishes his tail from side to side as he trails behind her. His stature barely fits through the opening, but he makes it work.

I thought he would have shifted into his man form by now, but he remains in full transition. From what I recall, he spoke of his hound side like it was a separate entity, a beast that lived within him. Could it be possible that this creature has taken over and refuses to grant him access back to his body? There's so much about this world I've yet to learn and part of me wonders if I'll ever have the answers to most of the questions that keep me awake at night. And then there's the other half that makes me consider if I want to know them at all.

Just when I start to make sense of something, everything changes. Is it even worth figuring out anymore? One thing is certain—we narrowly escaped death and I'm not confident it won't come creeping back in when we least expect it.

If the people who ran Rock Bridge resorted to killing every last demon that remained trapped within their walls, there's no telling the lengths they will go to ensure that all of the demons that got away meet that same fate, too.

"Dash," Wren's soft voice calls out to me.

I follow her into the large bathroom and nearly gasp at the sight of the massive shower.

She reaches inside and turns the dial. Water sprouts out from two different spots in the ceiling and then secondary streams flow out from about waist height. Steam immediately fogs the glass up.

"Can you help me?" She fumbles with the top of her shirt, refusing to use her other hand.

I step toward her and notice the bruising on her wrist. "Are you okay?"

She looks up at me, fresh tears welling in her eyes. "Not really."

How could I expect anyone to be okay after all that she's been through? All that I don't even know but can only assume. Rock Bridge is a terrible place, and the stories that float through the demon taverns only allude to the awful things that are done there.

Wren was no exception to that rule.

"I'm sorry," I tell her, because I'm not sure what else to possibly say. My heart thuds at the unknowns, the words I've wanted to tell her since she was taken that dreadful day. I begged the universe for this moment, to have her in front of me, and now I'm at a fucking loss.

"It's not your fault."

I swipe the hair off her shoulder and spot the fresh set of teeth marks near where Bo had marked her before. "Are those from Wes?"

Because if they were from anyone else, I may have to burn this entire realm to the fucking ground.

She nods faintly. "Dash?"

I slide her thick leather armored top over her shoulder, exposing her dirt-covered skin.

She slithers out of it not bothering to cover her now bare breast.

Still, I look away to give her as much privacy as possible in this vulnerable moment. "Yeah?" I slither the rest of the shirt over her other arm and lay it on the tiled ledge of the shower. I kneel before her and unbutton her pants, carefully dragging them over her ass.

"Do you still like me?"

Her question catches me off guard. "What?" Now it's my turn to look up at her. I steady her hands so she can step out of her pants and then stand.

"I just didn't know...if what happened...if it changed things between us."

"You can't be serious."

Wren averts her gaze momentarily, almost like she's embarrassed by the conversation. "I'd understand if it did."

I gently cup her battered cheek in my hand. "It only solidified the fact that I cannot live without you."

"Really?" A single teardrop rolls down her cheek.

I wipe it away with my thumb and kiss the spot where it had landed. "Really."

How could she possibly think anything else? Have I not made her feel secure in the way I feel about her? Have I grown so numb to things that my reactions have convinced her that I want nothing more than to be by her side until she will no longer allow it?

"You remained in every single thought of mine while you were gone. I begged the universe, the gods, the angels, anyone who might be listening to ensure your safety. Bo and I would have stopped at nothing to free you from that place."

"You two made it possible." Wren closes her eyes and leans into my touch. "We couldn't have done it without you."

I guide her backward and into the shower. "Here. I'll be waiting when you're done."

Her bright blue eyes meet mine. "Join me." She pauses and adds, "Please."

"Are you sure?" I ask her. There are no doubts in my mind about showering with her, especially after how the first time went, but I don't want to take advantage of a single moment if she isn't ready to be that close again. After all that's happened, she deserves some time to herself, too.

"Yes." She reaches for the hem of my shirt and tugs it upward with her good hand.

I drag the thing the rest of the way and toss it aside. I watch her step under the water and let it cascade down her face and over each delicate curve of her body while I remove the rest of my clothes. My cock throbs in response but is quickly hindered by the bruises and cuts scattering her precious form.

I thought Wes would have been able to heal her, to keep her out of harm's way, but I was sorely mistaken.

I join her in the stream of water and pull her to my chest, savoring the contact of our skin together. "I'm so sorry." I pat her hair out of her face and press my lips to her forehead.

"Will you kiss me?" She tilts her head up toward me.

How could I ever say no to her? I do as she wishes and melt my mouth onto hers, using the softest pressure I can possibly manage. I skim my tongue over hers and sigh in relief at being able to do this with her once again. I worried I had lost her forever, and here she is, in my arms.

Her hand trails down my shoulder, my arm, landing on my waist. She melts into me and picks up the intensity, her palm finding my shaft and gripping it in her small grasp.

My body betrays me and reacts immediately. "Wren..." I hold her face in between my hands and catch my breath.

"I want to feel anything else other than pain, Dash, please. I need this." Her gaze darts to something behind me. "You can come in here."

"Don't let me interrupt," Bo says from his spot in the doorway, not a hint of jealousy in his voice. He strolls over and puts his arm on the side of the shower opening. "But if you don't give the girl what she wants, I'll come in and do it for you."

Wren extends her hand out toward him. "Come on."

Bo exhales and remains in place. "You don't know what you're asking for, Birdie."

"I think I do." She motions for him to step inside with us. "Take your clothes off."

My heart increases its tempo as Bo complies. He kicks his pants off and walks under the other stream, letting it wash over his face. He runs his fingers through his long black hair and rings the water out.

Wren stands taller to kiss me, a new longing in each movement that wasn't there before.

I tug her body toward me and run my hands over the arch of her back and settle them on her plump ass. Dragging her off the floor, I lift her up and wrap her legs around my waist.

She reaches down and positions me at her entrance, stroking me with enough finesse that I'm surprised I haven't come undone yet.

"Are you sure?" I ask her.

"Just give her your cock already, Dash," Bo quips from his spot under the stream, his own cock gripped in his hand.

I try not to stare, but the sheer size of it makes me feel a bit lacking. I shift Wren slightly and settle her tight pussy over my shaft, penetrating her carefully. I moan and throb in a way I wasn't sure I'd get to experience when she was taken from us.

"You feel so good." Wren wraps her arms around my neck and glides her body up and down as best she can given her feeble condition.

I hold on under her thighs and move her gently.

She stops her motion and pulls away slightly. "Wes, is that you?"

I step backward and walk her over to the glass with my cock still buried inside her.

She wipes at the steam covering the partition and narrows her gaze. "Hey," she keeps her voice low.

"Plenty of room in here for all of us," Bo calls out from his spot.

I catch the darkness of Wes's fur out of the corner of

my eye and grow curious as to whether he will join us in his current form.

His hound whimpers and a moment later, the black coat is replaced by that of flesh.

I meet his gaze and worry for a second that he's going to rip my throat out for actively having sex with his fated mate, but if he hadn't done it while as a hound, chances are I'm probably safe from his immediate murder. I lower Wren onto the wet floor, allowing her to change her mind since Wes has joined us.

"Don't stop on my account." Wes steps into the shower, walking over to the open stream and tilting his head up toward it. The water pelts his face and chest.

I lean against the glass and wait for Wren to decide on what, or who, she wants to continue with.

She steps toward me and drags my face down onto hers, pressing her lips onto mine. She whimpers and drags her fingers up into my hair, tugging it in her fist.

When I open my eyes, Wes is behind her leaving a trail of kisses over her shoulder. He moves her hair aside and nips at her neck.

Wren lingers her own mouth down my jaw, onto my chest, and makes her way onto the tip of my cock. She licks the length and swirls her tongue over the end, dipping it under and taking me into her mouth.

I rest my head on the wall behind me and bask in the pleasure of being inside her in any capacity.

Wes enters her from behind, causing her lips to vibrate around my throbbing cock when she moans for him. He latches onto her hips and thrusts in and out of her, sending her rocking over my own shaft.

Wren tilts her head to the side, looking toward Bo. She reaches her good arm out and snaps her fingers, commanding him over to her.

He hesitates but complies, sauntering over with a lust-filled gaze.

Once he's within reach, she slides her mouth off me and spits into her hand. She takes me back inside her but uses the lubrication to grip onto Bo's enormousness.

Bo steadies himself on the wall next to him and focuses his attention on the tiny hand wrapped around his cock. He doesn't touch her, doesn't take anything more than she's willing to give. He could easily shove me out of the way and take my place, but instead, he's patient. Something that is so very unlike Bo.

I stop assessing the situation and concentrate on my own pleasure and experience with her. I bundle her hair off her face and hold it back, watching with bated breath as she consumes me. I feel myself heighten and like she senses it, her lips tighten and her tongue cups the bottom of my shaft.

She increases her suction and moans against me.

I explode in her mouth, not ready to be done but desperate for the release.

Wren doesn't pull away, yet she stays for the duration of my orgasm, sucking up every last drop I have to give her. Once she's satisfied I've reached completion, she hovers her mouth up my torso and returns to my lips, kissing me while Wes is inside her from behind and Bo is in her hand.

I reach between us and slide my fingers to her clit, applying gentle but firm pressure.

Her body quivers under the touch. She moans again and grazes her teeth over my bottom lip.

"Come for me," Wes whispers into her ear, sending her spiraling off the edge of bliss.

Wren falls into me, her lips still on mine, while Wes thrusts his own climax into her.

The two of them ride the wave together while I savor the up-close spectator's view of her pleasure.

Bo grunts and finishes right behind them.

Wren manages to continue stroking him through his orgasm while she comes down from hers.

She lays her head against my chest and continues to press her weight into me. I wrap my arms around her and cherish this moment, knowing that there's a chance it won't happen again. We may have escaped the clutches of Rock Bridge, but we haven't won this war.

19

WREN

I sit on the edge of the bed while Wes kneels at my feet and studies the wounds littering my body.

"What took you so long?" I ask him.

"To shift back?"

"That...and back at Rock Bridge. I thought you were dead."

He sighs and lowers his head. "I don't expect you to understand."

I place my finger under his chin and tilt it up to me. "It's hard if you don't talk to me."

Wes nods. "We have a lot to discuss."

I steady my wild nerves and say the thing I've needed to say since the moment it happened. "I'm sorry, that I..." I trace the remnants of the mark I left on his shoulder. "I shouldn't have done that."

His eyes light up, doing that glowing thing that sets

my soul at ease and lights it on fire at the same time. "Don't you apologize for that."

"You didn't consent to it, and I'll never forgive myself for doing it against your will."

"Against *my* will? Wren, I never wanted any of this for you. I didn't want you to feel obligated to be something you weren't. The mate bond that my hound formed with you, you never asked for that."

"Wes…"

He cuts me off. "It was wrong of me to pursue you. To put you in danger. To give in to my desires. To mark you."

"Wes…" I rest my palm along his cheek. "Wes," I say a little louder to get his attention. "You don't get it, do you?"

His jaw tenses and he blinks up at me. "What?"

"Why do you think I faltered that day in the warehouse? You've seen me fight; you know I'm not that sloppy. It was our bond latching into place and you can't convince me otherwise. I felt you before I saw you. But that moment my eyes locked on to you it was like waking from a deep sleep. I denied it. Damn, did I try. You and I both know there's no escaping what fate has in store for us. This connection that you're so convinced is one-sided…I feel every bit of it."

"That's not…possible." He stares at me, his eyes darting back and forth like he's trying to make sense of what I just told him.

I shrug and smile. "At this point, I'm convinced anything is possible."

"But you're a hunter." His statement comes across a bit questioning.

"Not anymore. Not the way I used to be. Never again."

Wes rests his head on my knees and kisses them. "Can I please heal you?"

Sighing, I consider his request. "Only a few things, because you need to stay strong for us, and if I'm being honest, I feel like shit."

"What hurts the most?" he asks me, his gaze expectant.

I hold out my wrist and turn it over. "This is more frustrating than all of them."

He brings it to his lips and mutters a few words I cannot decipher, the ache and pain dulling until it disappears completely. "Better?"

I twirl it around and bask in how fucking quickly that worked. "And how do *you* feel?"

"Totally fine, what else can I fix?"

I point down at my thigh, where I had Wes melt the wound shut to stop the bleeding.

"Lay back," he tells me.

I comply, relaxing my head on the plush comforter and savoring the touch of his lips on my skin. The pain temporarily increases, but then disappears completely. I prop myself up on my elbows. "Do you feel anything?"

He kisses the inside of my leg and trails his lips

down to another wound. "Not at all. And I should remind you, I cannot lie to you."

I flop back all the way and throw my arms out to the side. "Have at it then." Because frankly, I could use this kind of relief after the chaotic last few weeks.

Wes goes to work whispering sweet nothings to my body, healing the countless injuries I've sustained lately. With every wound mended, I feel my strength returning. A part of me wondered if I'd ever recover from the torment I'd experienced, but with Wes at my side, and Dash and Bo nearby, I have hope that maybe things won't always be bad.

He manages to cover the brunt of the wounds by the time Everest bursts through our bedroom door. "The house is on fire."

Bo and Dash both jump from their spots sprawled out on various pieces of furniture in the room.

"Are you fucking serious?" I ask him while hopping out of bed and rushing over to slide out of the sleep shorts I found in the closet and step into my armored pants.

"It's not hunters. It's demons." He rushes out and across the hall to pound on Tremont's door. "Sir, the house is on fire."

Tremont appears on the other side, his hair in a mess and his eyes half open. "What?"

"I repeat," Everest raises his voice loud enough for the entire place to hear. "We are under attack. The house is on fire!"

Bo steps behind me and tucks my hair behind my ear. "What's going on?"

Everest throws his hands in the air. "Oh, forget it, let's just all die."

"I'm just kidding." Bo ruffles the hair on Everest's head. "Where are your weapons?"

"Follow me." Everest takes off down the hall and into the front room, disappearing from our line of sight.

"It's got to be the wendigo army." I buckle the straps on my shirt and tuck the few knives I still had in my possession into various places on my body. "I'm not sure which is worse."

Dash tugs his shirt over his head and glances in the mirror. He walks over and kisses my cheek. "At least we're together this time." He points his finger at me. "No splitting up."

"Just try not to get killed."

Dash smirks. "I'll do my best."

We meet Everest, Bo, and Jade at the end of the hall.

"What's the plan?" I ask them, hoping someone has an answer. The last time I was in charge of something, it put all of us in danger.

Tremont lets out a breath. "Are we close to Folly?"

Everest nods. "Why?"

"There's a weak spot in the fold there. I assume it's under heavy guard, but if we can get there…" Tremont glances over at me briefly, it's not long, but long enough to send a chill down my spine. "We can cross-realm travel."

"That's not possible," I tell him. "The realms have been shut off for decades."

"And I've only been here a few years."

I stare at him, unsure of how he could be telling the truth. I recall Wes telling me this very thing, but to hear it directly from Tremont is a whole different story.

Wes speaks up. "It's our only shot, we have to take it."

"We don't have enough power to make it happen. Not for all of us." I count the bodies and note the juice that kind of travel would entail. From the minimal details I've read about the barrier put on our realm, this is simply inconceivable.

"What other choice do we have?" Tremont blinks around the group. "If it's not today, when? You can't run forever."

"Where will we go?"

"Wherever the angels send us." Tremont ducks as a flaming bottle bursts through the window in the kitchen.

It explodes, sending shards of glass flying by us.

Wes shields me with his body and pulls me toward him.

"We have to run, now." Everest latches onto Jade's hand. "If the hunters haven't caught onto our whereabouts yet, this could be our only chance out."

Even if we do make it to the vulnerable spot in the fold, we all won't be able to make it through. Someone is going to have to stay behind. Tremont is the magical creator of this plan so it's a given that he will go through. None of us will put Jade in harm's way, and there's no way Everest will leave her side. And after everything terrible I've done in my life, there's not a chance I'm willing to put myself above any of these three men I'm drawn to. It has to be me.

"I can't do a protective barrier this time. I have to save my power for the fold." Tremont clutches the knife Everest had given him.

Bo and Wes exchange a look.

Wes speaks for both of them, "We'll provide cover."

"I can help." I'm more than capable now that Wes healed many of my injuries. Not that having them would have stopped me either way.

"No." Bo grabs my hand and places it in Dash's on our way to the door. "You two stay together, do you hear me?"

"Don't you dare look at me with those goodbye eyes."

Bo scoffs. "There's no such thing."

"I'll clear a path, Everest, you lead the way." Wes grips the handle and turns to us. "Everyone ready?" He doesn't wait for an answer.

I kick off the floor and run behind Wes, being cautious of the flames that flicker off his body. I keep hold of Dash, mainly because I worry for his safety more than I do my own.

Wes remains in man form, but his beastly abilities surface. He blasts an orb of fire at an oncoming demon and sends them flying off into the bushes. Another approaches in front of him and he tosses a fireball their way, too.

I glance over my shoulder, Everest and Jade are on our heels, waiting for their opportunity to go around us.

Wes readies his arms to his side and lets out a ferocious roar, a wave of fire flowing out of his mouth and hands. The ground in front of him bursts into flames, killing anything in his path. The fire dies down and leaves nothing but a lingering smoke in its wake.

Everest uses the violent outburst to run ahead, leaving Jade near Tremont.

Dash glances over at me. "Do you trust him?" He tilts his head back at the man we know almost nothing about.

"Not really. Do you?"

Tremont could easily be running us straight into a trap right now and honestly, I wouldn't at all be surprised. Pissed, most definitely, but considering how things typically go for us, I wouldn't rule out that he isn't working for the enemy.

Not too long ago I thought these people around me were the enemy, and here I am, falling for three of them and fighting for the rest.

We leap over logs, run through briar bushes, and skid down a long slope.

My heart pounds so loud I can feel it in my ears, and a doom like no other creeps in. It's strange to be this out of control—to have nowhere safe to go. Every inch of this realm is plagued with vicious creatures that want nothing more than to kill us or steal our power.

Everest falls back, letting Wes take over, and joins Tremont at his side. "This is it, where to now?"

Tremont raises his hand and scans the air, running along the edge of the barrier keeping us trapped within Prania.

I swallow the thick lump that forms in my throat and look back in the direction we came. If the wendigo army catches up to us, we're stuck between them and an impossible boundary.

"I can't fucking find it." Tremont continues to investigate the integrity of the fold.

"Get behind me, Miss Oliver." Dash steps in front of me, a noble and kind gesture, but misplaced.

My fighting skills far outweigh his, and if anyone should be protecting anyone, I should be on the front line with Wes and Bo.

I didn't become *Furla Ain* for no reason. I earned that title—even if that role means nothing to me now.

"What did he call you?" Tremont steps in front of me and places his hand on my shoulder.

I shrug him off me. "What?"

"I was just teasing her," Dash says in what I assume is his way of trying to mediate the weirdness brought on by Tremont.

Tremont steadies his gaze, something wild and

disturbing about the way he's looking at me. "What is your full name?"

A battle cry sounds in the distance; a blaring alarm that our time is nearly up.

I reach to unsheathe two of my knives but Tremont insists.

"Your name, please. I'm begging you."

"Wren Oliver, why?"

His face turns white as a sheet and his mouth falls open. "Angels." Tremont latches onto my forearm and pulls me over to the fold. "We don't need a weak spot if we have you."

I yank at my arm. "Let go of me."

"I'm not trying to hurt you, Wren, I swear." He holds out his other hand to stop Bo and Wes from advancing on him, a flicker of magic sizzling across his palm. "Either everyone hold on or this train is leaving without you."

The screams of the army grow closer, and I figure, if I'm going to die, I'd rather it not be by some creature I accidentally embarrassed.

I grab onto Dash, linking his fingers around mine. "Come on."

Dash takes Everest's hand, who takes Jade's. Jade reaches for her brother, and finally Wes leads up the rear.

He blasts a steady current of fire at the ground to buy us a little more time from attack and turns to the rest of us. "This better fucking work."

"Hold on tight." Tremont steps to the barrier and hovers his palm against it. "Grant me access to your magic."

"My magic?" I stare at him. "I hope this whole thing doesn't depend on something that doesn't fucking exist."

But with the words I speak, something strange rattles in my core. The same thing I've felt numerous times in my life but have disregarded. The thing that blasted that magical device off my chest in Rock Bridge when Parla was trying to torture me. The thing that got me and Wes through the barrier when I went back for him and consumed too much of that poisonous fog. The thing that's kept me alive more times than I can count. A piece of me that I've never acknowledged until now, simmering just under the surface.

Tremont presses on the barrier keeping us trapped in this realm. A glaring light appears, beaming brighter and brighter until we're completely consumed by it. "Don't let go," he tells me over the deafening screams of the white energy.

Don't let go, I repeat to myself over and over, praying the rest of them can hear me.

Find out where Wren went in the final installment of her epic adventure in *Fated to Monsters*, book three in the *Falling for the Enemy* series.

Acknowledgments

To all the incredible people in my life, I adore each and every one of you. Thank you for being a part of this wonderful journey.

My mini me. My mom.

My bestie, Victoria.

My amazing assistant, Tiffany.

Sam Coleman and Michelle Marlow.

S.J. Fowler. Tori Ellis. Niki Trento.

Clayton. James. Tyler. Victoria.

To all of my readers.

Thank you.

About the Author

Luna Pierce is a paranormal and contemporary romance author who loves getting lost in her stories. She brings you tough characters that love fiercely and fight for what's right, even if that means burning the city down for the ones they love. Luna adores all things gritty, and even supernatural.

When she's not writing, you'll find her consuming way too much coffee, making endless to-do lists, and spending time with her daughter and cats in small-town Ohio.

Join the exclusive reader group: Luna Pierce's Gritty Romance Squad

Join Luna's newsletter to receive updates at:
www.lunapierce.com/subscribe

Also by Luna Pierce

Falling for the Enemy

Stolen by Monsters (Book One)

Fighting for Monsters (Book Two)

Fated to Monsters (Book Three)

The Harper Shadow Academy Series

(set in the same story universe as Falling for the Enemy)

Hidden Magic (Book One)

Cursed Magic (Book Two)

Wicked Magic (Book Three)

Ancient Magic (Book Four)

Sacred Magic (Book Five)

Harper Shadow Academy: Complete Box Set

Sinners and Angels Universe

(Dark contemporary romance)

Broken Like You (Standalone)

Untamed Vixen (Part One)

Villain Era (Part Two)